Cocktail

Lisa Alward

COCK

TAIL

STORIES

A John Metcalf Book

Biblioasis
WINDSOR, ONTARIO

FIRST EDITION
10 9 8 7 6 5 4 3 2 1

Library and Archives Canada Cataloguing in Publication
Title: Cocktail / Lisa Alward.
Names: Alward, Lisa, author.
Description: Short stories.
Identifiers: Canadiana (print) 20230156878 | Canadiana (ebook) 20230156916 |
    ISBN 9781771965620 (softcover) | ISBN 9781771965637 (EPUB)
Classification: LCC PS8601.L93 C63 2023 | DDC C813/.6—dc23

Edited by John Metcalf
Copyedited by Chandra Wohleber
Cover and text designed by Ingrid Paulson

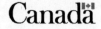

Published with the generous assistance of the Canada Council for the Arts,
which last year invested $153 million to bring the arts to Canadians throughout
the country, and the financial support of the Government of Canada. Biblioasis
also acknowledges the support of the Ontario Arts Council (OAC), an agency
of the Government of Ontario, which last year funded 1,709 individual artists
and 1,078 organizations in 204 communities across Ontario, for a total of
$52.1 million, and the contribution of the Government of Ontario through the
Ontario Book Publishing Tax Credit and Ontario Creates.

PRINTED AND BOUND IN CANADA

For my parents

Was there no safety? No learning by heart
of the ways of the world? No guide,
no shelter, but all was miracle, and leaping
from the pinnacle of a tower into the air?
VIRGINIA WOOLF, *To the Lighthouse*

Contents

Cocktail

THE PROBLEM WITH PARTIES, MY MOTHER SAYS, IS people don't drink enough. This is a joke. My mother is not a lush. Her fingers never shake when reaching for her coffee cup or laying down a trick at bridge. She doesn't ring up old friends at night, slurring into the mouthpiece, It's Marrrgo how arrre you? Like most of us these days, she sticks to wine—no more than a glass or two—or occasionally a beer in summer. Even the bottles of Grand Marnier and cassis that she used to bring out for special occasions, like my unexpected wedding at thirty-nine, are gathering dust in the sideboard now that both her own husbands are gone.

No, this is just her stock response to my complaints about going to parties, the ones where all the married couples stand in well-lit kitchens and talk about their vacations or their home renovations or the academic or athletic or toileting triumphs of their children. Her meaning is that if people drank more, they'd loosen up. Parties would be more fun, like they used to be. And I laugh along. Yes, I say, letting her top up my glass of Chardonnay. That's it, not enough booze.

But I'm thinking about Tom Collins.

MY PARENTS THREW A LOT OF PARTIES IN THE sixties. Everyone drank hard liquor (wine in those days was thought of as a dinner drink). In a cubbyhole of my father's desk once, I found the tally of expenses for the very first cocktail party they held in the house that I grew up in. These were, in descending order, neatly reflecting their priorities,

liquor $136
food $25
bartender $8
maid $5.

Next to the amount for bartender, my father had added in block letters TONY. For $8, this Tony, whom I remember standing at attention in a white jacket beside our blue Formica kitchen table, not only mixed and served the drinks but also did the purchasing based on his intimate acquaintance with my parents' cocktail set. These drinks had exotic and often slightly suggestive names, like Mai Tai, Sidecar, or Hanky-Panky, and they involved special ingredients and tools. In the door of our refrigerator, there were always jars of olives and pickled onions and red and green maraschino cherries. Extra ashtrays were stored in a cupboard above the sink, while another higher cupboard held the glasses: marble-bottomed Old Fashioned glasses, tall highball and even taller Collins glasses, delicate martini glasses with bowls splayed wide like spent tulips. A drawer in our telephone nook hid a collection of miniature plastic swords that my brother and I were not allowed to play with, as well as toothpicks with sparkly tassels, and packs of invitations. *Cocktails!* these small rectangular cards shouted in eager, crushed-together letters, the dot over the *i* a stuffed green olive or luscious red-stemmed cherry that I longed to pop into my mouth.

Sometimes my mother would let David and me watch as the first of her guests took off their coats, revealing dark suits with narrow lapels and dazzling shift-style dresses in emerald and tangerine. We always had to be sitting on the stairs, though, bathed and changed for bed, our teeth brushed, ready to turn and go the instant she gave the wave. Every time the door opened, I would tug my nightdress around my ankles and lean excitedly into my brother, who might be rapping a rolled-up comic book against his knee or clicking a pair of swords he'd snatched from the kitchen when Tony wasn't look-ing. But we never spoke to my parents' friends, even the ones we recognized as the mothers and fathers of our own friends, and my mother didn't introduce us. The cocktail party world lay at a remove: the grownups put on their party clothes and seemed to forget us. Cer-tainly, David and I knew not to come back downstairs

3

to fetch a glass of water from the kitchen or say we couldn't sleep, had had a bad dream. Instead, we lay under our covers thinking about the bared shoulders of the women, the stale cigarette smell that clung to the men's overcoats and listening to their voices: clinking and burbling at first, then swelling, seeming at times to almost rush against the floorboards. The harsh, sudden laughter that meant they were having fun.

At least, I listened. I never knew for sure what David did in his room across from mine. He was two years older and already sinking into the sullen impenetrability that would muffle him from us. Maybe he read his war comics inside the tent of his bedspread, a flashlight pointed at his knees. Sgt. Fury trapped in Hitler's Reichland: *Awright, you heroes! We got us a war to win!!* Or maybe he slept through the voices. The darkness between our two rooms was a river that only kept rising as the night wore on. It tore at my sheets, threatening to carry me out past the linen closet and the low hall bookcase, slowing briefly by the window that looked out on our yard, and then, before I could grab the banister or cry out, tossing me, like a leaf or a stick, down the narrow staircase to where I knew I shouldn't go—to where, even then, I didn't want to go.

I did go down once. I was ten or eleven and it was no longer the sixties. My parents' parties were changing. They started after our bedtime now and my mother put on records late at night: *Sgt. Pepper*, the soundtrack from *Hair* or *Easy Rider*. Instead of spending her day making tidbits on toothpicks from the *Joy of Cooking*, she often just filled bowls with Bugles or party nuts from a can. She had more time now to talk on the white push-button phone in her bedroom and even went out occasionally on party afternoons, leaving me with one of the ladies from City Sitters. Except for very large parties, my parents didn't bother hiring Tony anymore. They set out the liquor bottles and the mix, the jars of cherries and pickled onions, and people helped themselves. There was no maid either. In the mornings, David and I nudged aside glasses on the kitchen table to make room for our bowls of Froot Loops. We drank our Beep from tiny crystal sherry glasses, shaking these clean first in the sink. Then we watched Saturday-morning cartoons in the den until one of them came and found us, usually my father, looking oddly helpless in his wrinkled pajamas, his thin black hair sticking to the air.

That night I must have sleepwalked, reaching out to touch the sides of the stairwell on my way down. The nightmare was always the same: something was wrong, out of place. I would try opening my eyes wide, but the walls of my bedroom continued to expand and contract, rushing away from me, then pressing in again so fast I felt I might be crushed. It was as if there were some complicated adult problem I was expected to solve and even the walls were taunting me—but I was too young, I needed help. At the bottom of the stairs, I could see our telephone nook, its wooden shelf crowded with lip-smudged glasses and crumpled cocktail napkins. The party, though, had receded elsewhere, its din like the echo in a shell, blurry and contained. I wandered into the front hall, my feet gliding forward by themselves. Except for an evening purse, its long gold chain looped over a chair, the hall was empty. And yet not empty. In the small adjoining passageway that led to our powder room, a woman in a baby-blue hostess dress stood very close to a man in a grey suit.

The man was my Tom Collins, but I didn't know this yet. The woman was Mrs Goodwin. She had twin boys the same age as David (we called them the Goodwin Twins) and was often in our kitchen smoking when I came home from school. She also lent my mother novels: Book of the Month club ones with bold lettering and bored-looking couples on their scuffed paper jackets. Mrs Goodwin and the man in the grey suit didn't look bored though. The man's mouth drifted near her neck, and her face was flushed, gleaming with sweat, her breasts pushed up against the deep V-shaped opening in her dress.

I twitched for flight, but my feet were in control and this time stayed fastened to the rug. Anyway, it was too late. The man had seen me. He had a long, angular face covered in freckles, though his hair was brown, not red like mine. When our eyes met, the ends of his lips curved up as if there were some running joke between us. But I had never seen him before, not at any of the family skating parties or summer barbecues where I observed my parents' cocktail-party friends for longer than it took for them to take off their coats. Before I could look away, the powder room door swung open and my father staggered into the passageway. His suit jacket was missing and his white dress shirt starting to pull from his belt. In one hand, he held a crystal tumbler with some brown liquid at the bottom. He didn't see me and seemed only barely aware of the couple blocking his way as if he too were sleepwalking. Groping past Mrs Goodwin, he stumbled, his face sloshing forward with the liquid in the glass, and it was then that the man winked at me.

How I got to the den at the other end of the house I don't remember, only the reassuring glow of the table lamp as I stepped down onto its orange carpet. Someone else may have been in the room as well, but I can only picture my mother sitting in an armchair, relaxed and calm, as though she'd merely been reading a book in her cocktail dress, then smoothly rising to her feet. She must have shaken me, for the room shattered and all I could see were pieces of carpet and beige lampshade and my mother's gold earrings, the pale hollow in her throat. Then relief was filling me up like ice-cold water. Nothing was wrong after all. For here she was, gripping both my arms, and now my father was there too, looking on from behind her shoulder.

I was mistaken. Things were already moving out of place. Only a few months earlier, my mother had moved all her clothes into the guest room. Your father snores, she explained, and as my father's room took on more of the smell of shoe polish and Old Spice, it seemed as if they had always slept apart. My brother was also on the move, biking through distant neighbourhoods with the Goodwin Twins and, when he was home, retreating to his own room with family-sized bottles of Pepsi. *Here come the seventies*, bragged our television set on Thursday nights. Welcome to the Space Age, to the twenty-hour workweek, to no more teachers, no more books. I knew I should feel excited too, yet all this anticipation for what lay just ahead, the sense that life was about to become an endless party, worried me. Would every decade from now on have to have its own TV show? Lying on the den carpet, I would sometimes tighten all my muscles as if to stop the seventies from coming. But I could only hold on so long before I had to let go, my body flooding back into the room again.

FOR THERE WAS NO STOPPING ANY OF IT. TOM Collins showed me that the night he came upstairs. The knock was nothing more than a drunken finger tap. Then light was pouring in through a crack in my doorway and I could hear the party voices floating up the stairwell. I knew him from the freckles, though months had passed since the night my mother found me sleepwalking.

"Sorry," he said. "I was looking for the little boys' room. You know, just like the little girls' room but for—"

His lips curved the way they had downstairs when he'd tried to share the joke with me. "Wait, this is a little girl's room, isn't it?"

I sat up in my bed, pressed my back against its knotted wooden spools.

"The bathroom is downstairs," I said in my best approximation of the tone my mother used with pushy store clerks. But he didn't leave. Instead, he slipped through the crack of light into my room.

He was carrying a tall glass, which he settled behind him on a pile of library books on my dresser. He crossed one long leg in front of the other, rubbed his palms together, then reached back for his drink.

"What's that?" I asked, hoping I still sounded haughty.

"A Collins." He raised the glass and took a sip. "You want to try?"

I said nothing.

He gave an exaggerated shrug. "Your choice. But you're missing out on one of the most famous cocktails in all of history."

He swooped the glass toward me in a one-sided toast. Through its swirling liquid, I could see a maraschino cherry and a slice of orange and several melting ice cubes. "So, you want to hear why?"

I kept my face blank.

"Little girls like to hear stories, don't they?"

"I'm not a little girl."

"My mistake." He drew back in pretend embarrassment. "How old are you?"

"Fourteen," I lied.

"No, not a little girl then. Do you have a boyfriend?"

"No."

"Well, well." He paused to take another sip, and I inspected him more carefully. He was not handsome, his chin too small, his other features too fluid, and he was very thin, his shoulder blades propping up his suit jacket like a wire hanger. "Just make sure you don't wait too long," he said. "Or the boys might not wait for you."

"I don't care."

"Oh, you will in time. It's the nature of things, my girl, and there's nothing you can do about that. Nope. No escape. You can resist all you like, but one day some boy's going to catch you off your guard, pour you a little drink." He took yet another sip from his. "Whisper a little sweet talk in your ear, and bingo." He grinned. "Boyfriend."

No one had ever talked to me like this. Surely my parents wouldn't approve, even if he was their guest. I thought about calling out to my brother. But I knew David wouldn't hear unless I yelled.

"Don't be mad at me, Ginger," he said then, more softly.

No one had ever called me that before either. I found myself playing with a piece of my hair. I tangled it around my finger. He showed no sign of leaving.

"Tell me that story," I said. "The one about the drink."

"Ah, well, that's a good story. The Great Tom Collins Hoax. Ever hear of it? Nope? Well, I know you're going to like it. Are you ready? You sure? Okay, so you see, there was this guy in New York City named Tom Collins, a real loudmouth, and he was known for going into bars and saying stuff about people he'd just met and even stuff about people he hadn't met. A friend would come up to you and say, 'That Tom Collins, he just said you're a monkey's uncle,' or 'Thought you should know, Tom Collins is saying your mother wears combat boots.' And naturally you'd rush over to whatever bar Tom Collins was supposed to be in, ready to knock him down. But he wouldn't be there. He'd have moved on to the bar down the street or the bar around the corner, so you'd have to keep chasing him or drown your sorrows where you were. It even got into the papers, all these headlines about Tom Collins. *Last Seen on Fifty-Seventh Street!*"

He smirked and drank some more. "But turns out there was no such person. It was just a stunt by a liquor company to sell more booze."

I gave him my most withering look. "That's not much of a story."

"Good drink, though," he said, and drained the rest. He pulled the pieces of fruit out of the glass, peeling off the flesh of the orange slice with his teeth and handing me the bright red cherry. "Try it. Won't poison you, I promise."

The cherry tasted nothing like the ones on top of sundaes at Dairy Queen. Those were sweet. This one was unexpectedly sour, at least the skin. "What's in it?" I asked.

"Oh, you like, I see," he teased. "Two ounces gin, hint of lemon, teaspoon of sugar, ice cubes. Then soda water to the top of the glass. That's how you're supposed to make it, but your father buys the Collins mix. Not as good. Still—" He tipped the empty glass over on my carpet before placing it back on the dresser. "Not bad."

"Do you know my mother?" I asked, thinking of Mrs Goodwin in her hostess dress.

"Yes, I know your mother." His tone became cagey. "I know your mother and your father."

"How come I've never seen you then?"

"You've seen me, Ginger."

"I mean, before that."

"Well, maybe you've never snuck downstairs before."

I frowned and tried another tack. "Are you a friend of Mrs Goodwin's?"

He gave a low whistle. "What is this? The Spanish Inquisition? *They seek him here, they seek him there, that damned elusive Pimpernel!* You like to read, right?" He picked up one of the library books from my dresser. "What's this? *An Old-Fashioned Girl*? That looks way too babyish for a smart girl like you, a girl old enough to have a boyfriend. You should be reading the classics. Like *The Scarlet Pimpernel*. Or what about a modern writer, like John Updike or Philip Roth? Your parents have got a few of those downstairs."

He put my book down and swayed closer to the bed. "But to answer your question, a good question. It's like this, Ginger. People can be married. Like Mrs Goodwin, she's married to Mr Goodwin, and your mother is married to your father. And they can have a couple of cute kids and a nice house and a new car every two years and throw fun parties, even if they do settle for Collins mix. But all that, sometimes it just isn't enough. They want a little extra excitement. It doesn't mean anything."

"So Mr Goodwin knows about you and Mrs Goodwin?"

He laughed drily. "There's nothing to know."

"Why isn't it enough?"

He frowned. "You don't need to worry about any of this, you know, Ginger." He gave me a quick military salute. "The grownups have it all under control."

Then he leaned in further. I could smell his breath now and examine his freckles up close. They formed cloud-like splotches on his cheeks and some touched his lips. He seemed to be studying me too.

"So what's your real name, Ginger?" he asked with such gentleness I could feel my whole face go hot.

It was on my lips, mixing with the taste of the gin-soaked cherry, but before I could part them, David was standing inside my bedroom door. He had on his blue-striped pajama bottoms, and his skinny chest seemed to quiver in the crack of light.

"Who are you?"

The man straightened, stepped backward. "Relax, Junior. No harm done. We were just talking." He reached for his empty glass, raised it, and both hands, in mock surrender. "Good boy to watch out for your little sister like that. You're a lucky girl, Ginger. A lucky girl."

But I didn't feel lucky. I wished David had stayed sleeping, or whatever it was he did across the hall on party nights. I could tell what he thought: that that man was a creep. And I could see why he would think this, how it might be true—even as I wished the man wouldn't go, not yet.

Then, just as he was sliding past my brother in the doorway, he turned and winked again. "Tom," he said. "The name is Tom."

DAVID NEVER SAID A WORD ABOUT MY NIGHT visitor, to our parents or to me. Around that time, he stopped saying much of anything. When I think of my brother, his standing in that crack of light seems like a wooden plank thrown down across a silent waterway. Within a couple of years, he was gone—to California or Vancouver, we never knew. Just a note for my mother, *Sorry gotta go*, beside her empty wallet on the kitchen table. For awhile, I wondered if I would see Tom Collins at another of my parents' cocktail parties, but there weren't many after that. The Goodwins were the first of their friends to split up. Mrs Goodwin ran away to a hippie college in Toronto, where there really were no teachers and no books, and when she came back, she had a new man with her—not my Tom but a big-bearded psychiatrist who wore sandals and open-necked polyester shirts with knotted scarves.

Not long after this, my mother ran off with a friend of my father's she'd met at a bar convention do. I remember thinking that her leaving us was Mrs Goodwin's fault, that she'd been a bad influence with her Books-of-the-Month and low-cut dresses. But the wave of seventies divorces had only just begun. It was as if some force that had been dammed up had suddenly burst free and we were all churning in the undertow. Before long, everyone's parents seemed to be running off with their dentists or their secretaries or the spouses of their best friends. Or, like my father, drinking alone with the TV on, a cigarette dangling from his fingers, his ashtray the orange carpet.

Soon I had my own parties to worry about. These took place in basement rec rooms with fake wood panelling and built-in bars—unless no adults were home, in which case they spilled into ranch-style living rooms and dim kitchens and up more carpeted stairs into hall-ways and bedrooms and even bathrooms. Before these parties, my girlfriends and I chugged pints of vodka or lemon gin, chasing the taste that burned our throats with gulps of Pepsi or Orange Crush. Sometimes we stole from our parents, pouring into a jar a little from each bottle, then topping up this sort-of cocktail (we called it Moose Piss) with more pop. Soda water if we were desperate.

We drank to get with boys. To loosen our inhibitions so that we could walk up in our wide-leg jeans and key-hole sweaters and say, I'm *soooo* waaassted. Hoping that this would lead to necking on the stairs and then to whatever else it took to make us feel that we were hav-ing fun. Watch me walk a straight line, we'd call to one another, playacting that we were drunker, already looser than we were. Do you looove me? we sang at the top of our lungs. Will you looovve me forever? Then the boys' response: Oh, baby, baby, let me sleep on it. And when we zigzagged off the line, we'd all crack up, bending over with more laughter than we felt.

Occasionally I caught a glimpse of Tom Collins, in a lanky basketball star with freckles or a friend's wisecrack-ing older brother, the one who poked me in the cafeteria line to say, Hey, Ginger, see that chick over there, and when I looked, What she needs is a good fuck. But I knew my Tom would never be so crude. By the time I turned fourteen for real, our conversation in my bedroom had taken on the innocence of all that other *before time*—before high school and lemon gin and drinking parties.

Before my parents' divorce and dinners at the Ponderosa with my stepfather, his hand slipping inside my mother's blouse when he thought I wasn't looking. A time when men came to parties wearing suits and talked of books, when whatever roiled beneath the surface seemed held in check, channelled through locks, as if sex and all its risks were nothing more than an undulating canal, a drift of lips against a woman's neck. I never thought of him then as my seducer, but as my friend and protector, a gin-drinking guardian angel—though David was the one who'd come to my rescue (a detail that, along with David, I gradually let go of). Sometimes in my imaginings, my brother didn't come into my room at all that night. Instead, I told Tom Collins not just my name but also all the secrets of my mind until we tired of talking and he leaned closer still and kissed me lightly on the mouth. Or, if I'd been out drinking with the girls and wanted more, slipped under the covers in his grey suit and held me tight.

Even after high school, I was still looking for him, not seriously at first yet with a growing urgency, in college pubs and frat houses, in beer cellars and dance clubs and country-and-western bars. For fun, I bought a vintage cocktail dress and let anyone unzip it who wanted to. But it was Tom Collins's bony hips I always felt crushed against my own in the dark, Tom Collins's gin breath I tasted on my lips. I can't explain the allure he held for me, this inebriated party guest who stole upstairs to where the children were, for I no longer saw him as an angel—except that somehow his calling me a lucky girl got mixed up in the collapse of so much else. Don't worry, he'd said, the grownups have it all under control, and even then, I'd known this for a lie. Yet when I was smashed, which was becoming more and more, those long fingers holding out the cherry seemed a hint of sweetness. And I wanted to suck every bit of sweet from my glass.

If I was reeling out of control, I was too drunk now to care and so partied on, the seventies flowing into the eighties with surprisingly little excitement. But he was never there. Just when I thought I was getting close— some poet with unfashionably thin lapels, the accountant lingering over a liquid lunch at the table next to mine— I'd lose sight of him again. And find myself instead reaching for my clothes from yet another stranger's bed, the thudding of my temples as I re-hooked my bra and fished for my dress, a jeering reminder that I'd been fooled again. Until one sour morning-after, staring at a kitchen table lined with empty bottles, I saw him for the joke he'd always been, a boozy will-o'-the-wisp leading me on. A hollow clink of ice.

Old Growth

RAY'S REALTOR APPEARS TO HAVE NOTHING ON
from the waist up. She flashes across the front window
of her bungalow as if startled to see them drive into the
yard, though Ray did text her from the ferry. Gwyneth
glimpses shapely arms, a firm curve of breast.

"Your realtor's topless."

Ray leers across the steering wheel. "Whaaat?"

But it's just a nude T-shirt. Gwyneth can see this
plainly, now that the realtor has stepped outside in her
sock feet and is smiling at them, or rather at Ray. A tall
woman in her forties, reasonably slim with bushy blond
hair, the top piece pulled back in a faded green scrun-
chie. No doubt the younger and more attractive of the
two agents on the island: Ray would have done his
research.

Gwyneth considers making another crack but feels
chastened by the T-shirt. She's too late anyway. Ray has

flung open the driver's door and is loping across the grass to give his realtor one of the bear hugs he reserves for small children and pretty women. Gwyneth pushes her own door ajar and extends one sandalled foot, inspecting her toenails in the late-morning light. Purple, at her age, really? As she stands and unkinks her shoulders, Ray gives the blond woman a quick kiss near the mouth. Now the two of them glance over. This could be interesting. Is he going to introduce her as his ex-wife? Or as his friend, his adviser, his financier? Of course, he might just say she's a hitchhiker. This was how he introduced her to his parents all those years ago, and Gwyneth, twenty-four and in love, played along the whole weekend—though they'd met tree planting and Ray had gone to the bus station to get her.

"Fern," Ray says, "Gwyneth. Gwyneth, Fern."

Fern smiles limply. Then, brightening, she says to Ray, "Just give me a sec," and turns back to the bungalow where a pair of hiking boots wait beside a painted chair. She has a breathy little-girl voice, though on scrutiny looks closer to forty-nine than forty.

Gwyneth tries to catch Ray's eye, but he is gazing around his realtor's property: three acres with a vegetable garden, an orchard, and a pen for her horses (Fern gives riding lessons on the side). Gwyneth knows his air of distraction is deliberate, that he's already pulling away from their tenuous communion on the drive up the coast. If she speaks now, he won't hear, so intent will he be on communing with his realtor. Fern certainly seems flattered, pointing out the different types of apple trees and detailing the contents of the compost heap next to Ray's mud-splattered Focus.

Already, Gwyneth is regretting she's come.

I think I've found it, he announced on the phone. My land. And when she'd said, That's great, Ray, he surprised her by suggesting she drive to the island with him before he made his offer. They could get there and back in a day, and if they missed the last ferry, well, they could sleep in the car, like old times. Classic Ray. Yet he seemed so eager. C'mon, Gwyn. You can tell me if I'm crazy or not. And when she still hung back, I promise I'll be on my best behaviour. Neither of them mentioned the loan, but that's another reason he would want her to see it, so she'll feel easier giving him the $20,000, and on the phone, perversely, this touched her. Not that she cares which piece of wilderness he buys. She's already made up her mind to loan him the money—for Jenna and Gabe, so he'll have something to leave them, especially now that the cottage has finally sold and Ray is tearing through his share. It's your money. Ben had shrugged. But you know what he's like. As for doing a road trip with her ex-husband, he merely rolled his eyes. Maybe you can talk him out of it.

Ray at least was on time for once—early in fact. He appeared preoccupied with a roadmap while she was kissing Ben good-bye on the porch but smirked as she slid in beside him, Honeymoon still not over, I see. Then he lowered the driver's-side window and called out, Don't worry, man. I'll take good care of her. See you in two weeks! So that she had to reach across his skinny lap and shout, Tonight, Ben! See you tonight! As she eased back, she remarked, Still the same old asshole, I see, and Ray gave her a mock salute. But it seemed to relax them both, this allusion to a sexual rivalry that had never really existed. Ray being with Angie when Gwyneth met Ben.

Still, it felt strange sharing a car with him again. He'd started combing his hair back, she noticed, no doubt to camouflage his bald spot, and the light green hemp shirt he was wearing—short-sleeved with a collar and looking like it could use a little ironing—was one she'd bought a couple of months ago for Gabe to give him on Father's Day. In the store, she'd spent a long time fingering it, the fabric stiff like linen but with a hint of softness. So Ray. On the way out of the city, he detoured through a Tim's for coffees, and Gwyneth pulled back his tab and dabbed his jeans with their stack of napkins after he spilled the first sip. When Jenna texted, *How's your holiday with Dad? Killed him yet?* Gwyneth sent back a smiley face. But it was surprisingly relaxed, like catching up with an old friend. They talked about the kids: how great it was that Gabe was finally in a good place, and who was this new guy of Jenna's anyway? Also about Ben. (He's a good man, Ray said. Solid. You deserve that, Gwyn.) They even joked about a few of his more harmless flaws. How she still has to remind him about his mother's birthday and the time he drove six hours to his brother's wedding without his suit. Mainly, though, they talked about the land.

The seller, a middle-aged German, would be leaving behind a half-built house, and Ray was debating whether he should finish it or use the lumber for his own cabin in the woods. Why didn't the German finish his house? Gwyneth asked. No idea. Ray grinned. Maybe he got bored, or his marriage fell apart. Ray had spent much of his summer googling solar panels, composting toilets, organic gardening. A couple of pals were willing to help him build next year. In the meantime, he was hoping to find someone local (his realtor had a few names) to do the extra clearing he wanted. Then he would be able to quit his job and retire to the island, go off the grid. He looked at her with that intense light gaze, daring her to tear down this new plan. But that was one of the dispensations of being divorced so long: she felt no need to criticize, not anymore. Sounds great, she said. Then thought of the broken-down vw bus he'd bought for five hundred dollars and left to rust in their driveway, the treehouse he was always going to build the kids, all those rotting boards behind the garage. You're going to love it, Ray enthused, rapping the steering wheel. Wait till you see all the old growth.

FERN WON'T STOP GOING ON ABOUT THE TREES either.

"Wait until you see the old-growth firs on Ray's land," she says, catching Gwyneth's eye in the rearview mirror as if signalling her to gush as well.

They have switched to the realtor's Outback and Gwyneth is already feeling carsick. Not only is she trapped in the backseat, but Fern keeps taking her hands off the wheel to talk, then jerking the wheel back in place to round another bend. Gwyneth wonders if calling the land Ray's before he's put in an offer is an old real estate trick. Even Ray is doing it now, worrying aloud that the farmer next door to his land might be tapping *his* maples.

When they first set out from the bungalow, she'd made a point of asking Fern questions about herself. The realtor explained that she was born on the island, as were both her grannies, but that her parents left for the mainland in their teens, only to return with the back-to-the-land movement in the mid-seventies. Up until Fern was eight, they lived on a communal farm with two other families. She was home-schooled, but mostly she ran wild in the woods. Ray would like that, Gwyneth reflected. He'd always considered himself a latter-day hippie and often seemed dazed by their mortgage, the kids, his job teaching communications to blasé college students. Fern got along beautifully with the island's other realtor (who made pottery on the side), and, no, she didn't know why the German had abandoned his house. When Gwyneth asked about her horses, she boasted that she'd been riding since she was three. That's a long time, Gwyneth said, but Fern laughed: I'm not that old. She kept waiting for Fern to ask her something back. Surely she must be wondering why Ray brought along this definitely old-already woman with the purple toenails. But the realtor seemed no more curious about her than did the dusty ostrich ferns lining the ditches.

Gwyneth now directs a question at Ray. "Have you looked into the water supply?"

"Oh, he doesn't need to worry about that. There's good access to groundwater everywhere on the island."

"Gwyneth's partner's a civil engineer," Ray remarks, though he knows full well that Ben's a tax lawyer.

"Are you okay?" Fern says into the mirror.

"I'm fine. I'm just feeling a little carsick."

"Well, make sure you tell us if there's anything we can do to make you feel better," she says cheerfully, turning back to Ray to chat about his new neighbourhood as Ray surveys the dense bush on either side of the highway with childlike wonder.

When she finally pulls over, asserting with an excited flick of the hand, "Here we are!" there's nothing to suggest they are anywhere, certainly no *For Sale* sign.

Fern hops out of the Outback and points to a stick smeared with pink paint. "The western marker for your property line, Ray."

Next, she unfurls a survey map that shows how the eight acres begin narrow, then widen near the house before narrowing again for four more acres. Ray, of course, has seen the land before (this clearly is how he's become so cozy with his realtor), but he frowns at the map and stares blankly at Fern as though he's forgotten who she is or why he's here. Gwyneth, who's seen him like this before, guesses he's starting to feel nervous about the prospect of going off-grid for real. Commitment has never been Ray's forte.

Fern doesn't seem to notice and leaps into the ditch. As Ray plunges in after her, he throws Gwyneth a quick backward grimace. "You coming?"

"You bet!"

On the phone, she did think to ask about footwear. Would sandals be okay? Yes, yes, he'd assured her. The German had dug a road in from the highway. But Fern must have decided to take an off-road route.

"You okay?" she calls over her shoulder.

Huge rubbery leaves slap Gwyneth in the face. Bark grit jams beneath her toes. "Just fine."

Up ahead, Ray has regained his composure and is tilting his head close to his realtor's as she regales him about the natural attributes of his land. In addition to being a real estate agent and riding instructor, Fern appears to have an exhaustive knowledge of island flora and fauna. She is practically running now, showing off this big-leaf maple and that rare forest flower, noting how interesting it is that a cedar has rooted itself around the stump of a fir. She is quite the nature girl. No doubt she also leads a Brownie troupe on the side. Ray, though, Gwyneth observes with grumpy satisfaction, is even balder than she realized.

"Look at this, Ray."

Fern has stopped beside an enormous fallen tree. Someone has chain-sawed it into chunks, the largest spanning almost four feet. She nudges Ray's elbow, beckons Gwyneth.

"See the rings," she says, pointing at the largest chunk. "You can tell how old it is by counting them." Definitely a Brownie troupe.

Now she's caressing the outer rings with her fingertips, and Gwyneth worries that she might actually begin to count them. Instead, she steps back, her yellow pony-tail grazing Ray's hemp shirt.

"The rings look pretty much the same until you get right up close. Then you can see that some are wider, meaning an easy winter and long growing season, and some thinner, usually a hard winter and shorter grow-ing season."

"Like relationships," Ray quips, "except the best ones are usually the shortest."

Even Ray seems puzzled by what he's just said.

Since he and Fern are still hovering by the rings, Gwyneth sits on one of the smaller chunks of sawed tree and flaps her cardigan at the mosquitoes. She's promised herself that she won't think about Angie anymore. But the rings remind her. Once, at a family bonfire, she watched Ray and Angie hovering like this—not talking or touching, just standing near one another, and yet the force of their attraction cutting her to pieces. *You know he's not monogamous?* his own brother warned her. She knew, but married him anyway. Watching Fern try to make sense of the joke about the rings, Gwyneth feels sorry for her. It's Ray who turns her into such a bitch—even now when there's nothing between them but their almost-grown children, and this loan. Why should she care anymore who he screws around with? She's supposed to be done with all that, starting over with Ben.

But he still gets to her. She should have known this. She did know. All the time they were talking in the car, on the phone as well, she'd been softening, feeling the nearness of the old Ray—the one who kissed her breasts before babies, who was always floating off somewhere but still could always make her laugh. Even the wrinkled hemp shirt is a tendril, pulling her back. But she'd been a fool to think he wore it for her.

She heaves herself up. "Are we anywhere near the road yet?"

"It's just ahead," Fern sings out.

THE ROAD IS NOTHING BUT A GRASSY PAIR OF old tire tracks and the house, when it at last materializes, weirdly narrow with a tin roof that juts out so far that the two storeys look in danger of tipping over. Beside the house sits a leaf-strewn camper van and in front a rusted pickup truck. The whole scene has a haphazard sleepiness, as if the German has merely gone out for supplies and forgotten to come back.

Now that they've reached their destination, Ray seems about to break into a jig. "What do you think?"

"What's with the roof?" Gwyneth asks.

"We think he must have been planning to build two screened-in porches, one on top of the other," Fern says. "That's why it's so extended in front."

"And is that the only door?' Gwyneth points up at a large triangular opening.

"Oh, no." Fern laughs. "We think that was meant to be a door to the upper porch. The main door's around the side."

Ray and Fern stride ahead, murmuring back and forth, while Gwyneth picks her way through the nails and shards of wood littering the long grass. She has wrapped her cardigan around her head to keep away the bugs and knows without looking that the purple polish is all chipped now.

Inside the house, Ray becomes suddenly attentive again, showing her a table full of good-quality tools the German left behind and cautioning her, as they climb the rough stairs to the second floor, to stick to the cross-beams and not stand too close to that hole in the outer wall. He is especially proud of a curious window that shutters from the inside and can be opened only by pulling across a wooden stick. This stick is about two feet long and carved at one end with leaves and flowers. It is the one detail of the house that is truly finished.

"It's beautiful, isn't it?" Fern whispers, fingering a petal, and Ray looks at Gwyneth.

His appeal is so palpable she can't at first respond. Instead, she glances over the edge of the gaping triangle, which in that moment strikes her as a perfect metaphor for their unfinished marriage. Large flakes of brown paint are starting to drift loose from the cab of the German's truck. Nearby, a plastic tarp clings by blue threads to a pile of mossy lumber. The tarp reminds her of Ray's faded one-man tent from their tree-planting summer. There's something about me you need to know, he told her the first night she shared it with him. I just blow with the wind. I can't help it. Tangled up inside his sleeping bag with the shadows of the treetops moving above, she hadn't understood, or cared much, what this blowing might mean. She only knew that she wanted to curl herself around his body, so thin and pale in the tent light, and not let go. I think I'm in love with you, he also said, lifting her bangs. And she'd felt sure he meant it, because he looked so surprised.

Gwyneth sighs and faces him again. The German was clearly insane. She can't believe Ray is considering finishing the man's house. It will take him years, if he manages to even stick with it. Really, Ben was right. The idea of his going off-grid is ridiculous—what does Ray know about organic gardening? She watches him toss a screwdriver of the German's from one hand to the other, his pale blue eyes fixed on her, wanting her to say something nice about a carved stick. What is she even doing here? He must know she lacks his realtor's breezy confidence that he can pull this off. And if he's concerned about the money, why risk her seeing the land, or for that matter seeing him with Fern?

Then it all just seems so obvious. He's as stuck as she is. Even now, he can't make a move without turning back to see if she will try to stop him. Some free spirit—more a tangled kite, twisting along the ground. For the first time all day, she feels like laughing.

"Nice workmanship," she says, and when Fern asks what she thinks of the rest of the house, she smiles sweetly. "I think it has real potential."

Fern wants to take Ray to see the very end of the property. Gwyneth says she is still a little carsick and would rather wait. Against the side of the house, they find her a bench—just a narrow workbench pocked with ant holes, though she insists it's perfect. They both seem to want her permission to leave, Fern asking a couple more times if she's sure she'll be okay. But she smiles and waves them into wilderness. When she can't hear their voices, she lies back on the bench. Ray's trees are shifting overhead as if preparing to uproot themselves and walk away. Not that they can, any more than Ray. She pictures the two of them out on his land, the giant ferns gently stroking their bare arms, not talking so much now. Ray will be watching for a spot where the ground is soft, where he can pull her down. Or maybe Fern, impatient for his touch, will seize his hand and press him against an ancient maple. Let them do it. She wants them to. Let him add another ring. Even if they forget all about her, desert her on this bench by the mad German's half-house, it will make no difference. The sun can go down, the air turn chill, the house cave in behind her. She'll be waiting here for him.

Hawthorne Yellow

ONE NIGHT, ABOUT SIX MONTHS AFTER THEY
moved in, James got so mad at Tracey for nagging him
about the guest room that he charged upstairs with a
steak knife and started hacking at the walls. The only
apology she'd receive was a terse email: *Hired painter,
starts Wednesday, will do stripping—J.* It was waiting for
her when she finished putting Nicholas down for his
nap the next morning, the mail icon on their six-year-
old Mac flashing officiously at her from the alcove at the
top of the stairs. She didn't bother writing back. Instead,
she carried on down the hall and stood in the doorway
again to brood on the wallpaper.

The background was a drab ivory, stained yellow in
places, while the large silver flowers that ran across it in
diagonal rows were rubbery to the touch, like the daisy
bathtub stickers so ubiquitous in the seventies. Except
those flowers at least had been cheerful. These reminded

her more of Venus flytraps, each stylized petal an elongated tongue lined with feathery teeth. And now there were all these gouges in them from the knife.

She could have just done the room herself, of course. Apart from the bathroom, it was the smallest, ten-by-six feet, with only a single narrow window. Sara, James's friend at work, had just repainted her kitchen for the second time (the undertone of the first shade had been too yellow), and the women in Tracey's mothers' group always seemed to be taking on solo home improvement projects, though their houses were much newer and seemed, to Tracey anyway, already perfect. But even the thought of taping baseboards made her hands perspire.

It was supposed to be their dream house: an Edwardian detached that needed work but with what Sara, who'd recently purchased a Queen Anne two streets over, described as good bones. These included a double parlour with its original wide-planked softwood floor, a pantry off the dining room, and a set of kitchen stairs. In the beginning, Tracey had pictured herself and James lovingly restoring the old house together, long hours spent stripping and crack filling and painting like the sunlit couples on the line-of-credit flyers. But Nicholas was colicky those first few months, requiring her to carry him almost constantly, so James had had to do the double parlour on his own. He'd figured he could knock it off in an evening or two, only the dingy blue turned out to be painted-over wallpaper and underneath that were five more equally stubborn layers. By the time the stripping was done, he was understandably exhausted, but although a big project at the office got in the way, he did eventually paint all four sides of the room. All he'd done on the house since, however, was forage in big-box stores for special screws or drill bits that then just sat around in their packets on the kitchen counter.

Tracey crossed to the guest room window and gazed down at the overgrown yard, a familiar panic rising into her fingers on the sill. It wasn't just his email, or even the steak knife—she was getting used to scenes. It was the house itself. She kept having dreams where she discovered extra rooms that their realtor (who sometimes merged with Sara) hadn't shown them. Once an entire attic floor with old-fashioned spool beds set at odd angles and a rocking horse with coarse beige hair; someone else's children's clothes spilling out of the dresser drawers. It'll be okay, she'd tell herself in the morning. She could deal with all that stuff later, though even when she was fully awake, these hidden furnished rooms weighed on her mind, making her feel as if she were an imposter, an intruder, and the old house knew it. That James would just go hire someone after insisting for so long that he'd do the work himself was infuriating, yet all she could feel at the window, with those grim silver flowers massing out behind her, was relief.

JAMES'S PAINTER CAME A FULL HOUR EARLIER than expected. Tracey was still wearing baggy maternity leggings and a spit-up-stained T-shirt, Nicholas fussing over his pureed apricot. She knew she was being rude when she opened the door only partway.

"My husband said nine."

He was a smallish man, probably in his mid-forties, with greying black hair shaved close to his skull and the remote, self-contained air of a Tibetan monk. There was something almost too bright, too deliberate about his white coveralls as if he'd dressed the part, or been dressed for it by someone else.

"I start at eight." His breath smelled of minty gum. He gestured toward the driveway. "Am I okay there?"

She expected a truck, white like the coveralls, but it was just an old Volvo with the backseat let down, stuffed with drop cloths, a speckled metal stepladder.

"That's fine," she said.

Behind her, Nicholas was no longer simply fussing. Instead, she heard the hiccuping gasps that meant he was rising out of the high chair, chubby knees clenched in fury.

"Excuse me," she said.

But the cupboards were already splattered with gleaming orange spots.

Pausing in the guest room doorway some time later, her baby on her hip, she saw that the steak knife was now lying on the windowsill and that the strips of paper James had gouged from the walls while she screamed at him to stop had been neatly brushed into a dustpan. Arranged in a row on the floor were several putty knives as well as a bucket filled with water from the bathroom and a ripped-open package of blue and pink sponges. The painter must have sensed her in the doorway but continued wetting the back wall. From what she could see through the slits in his coveralls, he was remarkably trim for his age (even James at thirty-two had begun to soften around the middle). His neck and arms were also very tanned. From painting outdoors, she supposed.

She cleared her throat. "How's it going?"

He turned so slowly it flicked through her mind that he might be high.

"Well," he said, not meeting her eye, "I'm afraid it's a bigger job than your husband thought." He delivered a series of abrupt statements into the hall. "You've got about four layers. A couple are painted over. I'll need to rent a steamer. This is the original plaster, so it's going to be messy. You'll want to keep the baby away. I'll have to do some crack filling, which will need to dry. I can get the paint at a contractor's discount. You'll have to reimburse me for the steamer."

"Fine. My name is Tracey, by the way."

"Alex," he said, turning back to the wall.

From Nicholas's room, she could hear the slosh of the sponge in his bucket, then the quick jabs of a putty knife. She found herself putting more energy than usual into *The Cat in the Hat*. Her voice sounded loud and affected, which made her feel stupid as if she were play-acting at mothering, then angry again at James. How did he expect her to go about her normal routines with that man in the house? But Nicholas had fallen asleep in her arms and there was nothing she could do but slide back and forth in the rocking chair and listen to James's painter scrape.

THE NEXT MORNING, SHE SHOWERED EARLIER than usual, put on a sundress and her new sandals with the wedge heels, even a little makeup. Once the painter arrived, she'd decided, she would take Nicholas in the stroller to the playground. Stay out of the man's way for a good part of the day.

But the bell didn't ring until after eleven. She could smell cigarette under the gum this time, and he wasn't wearing the coveralls, just a sleeveless shirt and paint-flecked jeans, ripped open at the knees.

"I thought you started at eight."

"Had to get this." He held up what looked like a plastic toolbox with a hose attached.

By the time she reached the playground, it was nearing twelve and Nicholas already getting cranky. The one other mother still there, sensibly dressed in capris and a long-sleeved cotton T-shirt, was pushing two older girls in pink bucket sunhats on the swings. Tracey had forgotten Nicholas's ball cap at the door. She made a show of vigorously smoothing sunscreen on his cheeks but knew she looked careless, overdressed.

As she coaxed him down the slide, she heard herself using the same overly loud Dr. Seuss voice from the day before. "Look at you go, Nicky! Good boy!"

Nicholas wanted to swing too. Yet as soon as Tracey carried him over and threaded his feet through the openings in the baby seat, his head lolled to one side.

"Time to go home, Nicky," she said. "Time for lunch." But when she tried to pull him out, he rammed both his legs straight.

"Looks like someone missed his nap," the other mother remarked serenely, her two swinging daughters looking on from underneath their matching sunhats. And as Tracey hauled him up by the arms and clamped him kicking and wailing into the stroller, she added, "Poor little fellow."

Naturally, on the walk home, he fell asleep. In the yard, Tracey managed to undo the plastic clasp that held the four stroller straps together and gently slip her hands underneath his limp torso without waking him. Coming inside, though, they were greeted by a harsh rasping sound, like a boiled-dry kettle, and Nicholas immediately squirmed in her arms. When she strapped him into the high chair for his lunch, he fussed to get out, then wouldn't go down for a nap. She tried her and James's room, which was the farthest from the steamer noise, but he only rolled about on their brass bed, wrecking the nest of pillows and stuffed animals she'd so carefully arranged. Finally, she set him down in just his diaper on the floor of the double parlour and put on a video of Golden Age cartoons (a gift from her mother that James didn't consider age-appropriate).

Fetching a clean soother (another concession her husband disapproved of), she stopped in the guest room doorway. The painter had opened the window as high as the sash would go, but the room felt stifling. He was inching the steamer paddle up the back wall, his shoulders and arms beaded with sweat. For a man just shy of medium height, his hands were quite large, paw-like, the fingers blunt. On his right wrist, he wore a chunky stainless-steel watch. For some reason, she couldn't take her eyes off the wristband of this watch. The sight soothed her, making her feel that everything was under control, that the room would get done. Nicholas settle, as the books all said he would. She and James get back to normal. Yet when Alex turned this time, he gave her such a wary look. He must be used to this, she realized: married women spying on him from doorways. And maybe over the years some had come on to him, lightly touching a bare shoulder or even slipping a hand underneath that sleeveless shirt. What did he think? That she wanted to do it on a drop cloth while her ten-month-old watched cartoons? He could be as old as fifty. All the same, she felt exposed, as if he'd just told her she couldn't do that.

When he finished for the day, she was talking to James on the phone. James kept telling her to keep her voice down, which she knew had to do with Sara in the cubicle next to his—as if it mattered what Sara heard. Except it did. Marriage, she was discovering, a kind of show house where everything had to look just so. At least Nicholas looked happy for a change. A drooling Buddha, he reached out damp fingers, showing her the beeping bird on the cliff's edge. From the front hall, Tracey could hear Alex pulling on his work boots and grasping the door handle with the same delicacy she imagined Sara employing to sift through papers on the other side of a dividing wall. Then she just didn't care. She laid into James anyway as Wile E. Coyote wheeled through the air.

THAT NIGHT, SHE HAD ANOTHER HOUSE DREAM. Instead of discovering rooms full of other people's stuff, she floated down the main stairs and out the front door to the porch. Their brass bed was parked in the driveway. James was sitting on it in only his jockey shorts while Sara, wearing a silk blouse and black pencil skirt, lay on her side facing him. They appeared to be doing work. File folders were strewn about, a black push-button office phone balanced on a pillow. James held a lit cigarette in one hand, which also made no sense as he'd been the one to insist Tracey stop her casual smoking at parties (a dirty habit, he'd called it). So she looked again, and this time it was Alex on the bed with Sara, and he was naked, which jarred her awake like a door slamming shut in an empty house.

In the morning, she taped a note to the mailbox and left a key under the mat. She walked Nicholas to the playground and then to Shoppers to pick up a few things and finally to the Second Cup, where he napped in the stroller and she leafed through an issue of *Traditional Home*, relieved for the moment to be out of her own one.

But eventually she had to go back to give Nicholas his lunch. She stowed the stroller in the yard again, changing his diaper on the grass to avoid having to go upstairs. In the kitchen, she didn't hear anything from above though. He must be on his lunch break, she decided. Probably he'd been sitting in the Volvo as she walked by with the stroller and she just didn't notice from the sidewalk. She pictured him undoing a sandwich from its tight layers of plastic wrap, pulling back the tab on a can of pop, and when he was finished eating, rolling down the window to tap his ash onto their driveway.

But he wasn't outside. While she was cutting cheese into baby-sized cubes, he poked his head out the kitchen stairwell.

"Tracey?"

Her hand holding the knife jumped. "Oh, you scared me." It was the first time he'd used her name.

"Sorry. Can you come up?"

He seemed to want her to come right away, so she lifted Nicholas out of the high chair onto her hip and put a cracker in his hand.

More than half the room had been stripped, and the exposed plaster shone dully where he'd wiped it down. An open garbage bag swelled with torn pieces of the silver-flowered wallpaper as well as a thicker paper covered in mauve paint and another painted mustard yellow. Also a fourth, surprisingly pretty paper featuring miniature pink rosebuds on a white background.

"Do you see her?"

At first, all she could make out was a sea of damp plaster and, to the right, a rough silver shoreline running from ceiling to floor and peeled back in places to reveal patches of mauve. As she kept staring at the plaster side of this shoreline, though, a mat of black lines emerged.

"It's a woman," he said.

And now she could see that the matted lines were meant to represent hair and a thicker curving line the outline of a cheek and chin; that one of the mauve patches hid the corner of one eye.

"Look, Nicky. Someone's drawn a picture of a woman on the wall."

She guided Nicholas's hand to the woman's cheek, then touched it herself, the plaster as smooth, as soft almost as real skin. But these were just surface movements. They barely felt real. Underneath, she was only aware of Alex's body next to hers.

"Who do you think drew her?" she asked. His skin smelled of ash and sweat.

"A workman maybe? What do you know about the people who built the house?"

She tried to visualize the surname from the deed. She'd been vaguely interested in the lawyer's office. But he was too close, Nicholas too heavy in her arms.

"I don't know anything," she said, dropping to the floor to prop Nicholas against the wall, then wiping her baby's mouth, gummy with cracker, with her fingers.

Alex was looking down at her, the wariness all gone. His eyes, she noticed, were very brown. A curiosity radiated from them, a warmth, making her think she hadn't really seen him properly before, that even in the ripped jeans he'd been bundled up.

"It's charcoal," he said. "But they didn't paint over it. They just covered it with this."

He plucked a scrap of the older, prettier flowered paper from the garbage bag and crouched to lay it on her palm.

THE REST OF THE AFTERNOON, SHE STRAINED TO hear him wherever she was in the house. She imagined his cheek next to the guest room wall, chipping ever so lightly so as not to hurt the drawing, maybe using his hands, rubbing the sodden paper into tiny balls. When he left for the day, Nicholas was on the changing table and Alex padded downstairs so quietly she felt uncomfortable calling out.

The woman was now fully revealed at least. She had very large close-together eyes, thickly outlined like ancient Egyptian eyes done in kohl, and a long thin nose with slightly flared nostrils, while her hair was piled up in a dense, messy bun. Here and there were dabs of colour. Blue strands in the barely tamed hair. Fleshy orange in her nose and lips. Another hint of blue in the cameo brooch on the high ruffled collar of her blouse. These gave the drawing a rushed, almost careless quality, yet it was strangely arresting, modern even. The woman's head and shoulders present in the tiny room in a manner that seemed at odds with her Victorian clothing. All these years she had been covered up, hidden underneath wallpaper and paint. The idea of all those layers being peeled away made Tracey shiver. She couldn't wait to show James.

HAWTHORNE YELLOW

Somehow, in the confusion of supper and Nicholas's bedtime, though, she forgot to.

Later, curled behind her husband's sleeping back, she thought about Alex's hand on the putty knife. Suddenly, she was feeling his hand between her legs, the same sure rhythm moving up and down, and she came almost without touching herself, only the lightest brush of fingers.

THAT WAS FRIDAY. THEN CAME THE WEEKEND AND groceries and the vacuuming and Nicholas's tiny-tots swim class and a date night with James. Except she kept ending up in that room. It was as if the house had settled overnight, all the floors become tilted in this one direction. She would nip upstairs for Nicholas's diaper bag or to rummage through her bathroom drawer for a lipstick and find herself staring again at the woman on the wall and then at Alex's bucket, his line of putty knives, the dustpan coated with plaster dust.

Then came Monday and her mothers' group. She took another early shower, threw in a wash of crusty baby clothes, unloaded the dishwasher, rushed Nicholas through his breakfast. Yet even the sound of the door-bell made her wet.

That it was just physical was obvious. The longest speech she'd heard him make was the one about the steamer. She didn't know a thing about him. Not even how James found him. Or if he had a girlfriend or was married but just didn't wear a ring. What she did know was that her own marriage was going through a rough patch. Perfectly normal, the books all said, and why they recommended the date nights that were starting to feel like just another chore to nag James about. And for what? So they could drink wine in a restaurant and talk about his work. How they would arrange things once she went back to hers. What more they should do to the house. The truth was that when Alex grazed her palm with the wallpaper scrap, she'd felt not just the dry heat of his fingers and her own surprised pleasure, but also, deep inside, a booming emptiness, like a dryer going through its cycle with nothing but some dishrags or a lone slipper.

Nicholas was making a steamer noise as he pushed Cheerios about on his tray. Tracey filled his sippy cup with apple juice and nestled it inside her diaper bag with the two extra Pampers and tin of diaper cream, a torn-open pouch of wipes. Should she go upstairs and tell Alex they were leaving?

But she didn't have to, for here he was, leaning out of the kitchen stairwell again and saying her name in that same sweetly tenuous way, asking her to come up.

She left Nicholas in the high chair this time. He was strapped in after all.

"I've found another one," Alex explained, half turning on the narrow stairs.

He'd done a much rougher job with the stripping this time, yet the second drawing was clearly visible, to the left and a little below the first. The bust of a young man with high cheekbones and long wavy hair falling loose to his shoulders, the open collar of a shirt revealing not just his throat but a few strands of curling chest hair. And scrawled beneath a year, 1904.

"That's when the house was built," she volunteered. "My husband thinks this must have been a servant girl's room. Because of the stairs."

Once she'd shown her to him, James had taken quite a proprietorial interest in the woman, tracking down the name of the house's original family, which was McKay, and speculating that they were likely members of the Scottish merchant class.

"I don't think that's your servant girl," Alex said.

"She's the lady of the house, isn't she?" A foolish phrase. She blushed.

"Yeah, she could be." Then he smiled. "The guy looks like a rock star."

And she smiled back. "Oh, you're right. He does."

They were standing so close that they could have easily touched without entirely meaning to. She missed that, she realized, touching a man for the first time. Kissing him. The sharpness of his chin, his nose. That newness. The way it always made her feel new too, conscious of her own angles, but also her suppleness, how she could make herself fit. Then one of them must have swayed, for somehow her right shoulder was pressed just below Alex's left bicep, his flesh firm and warm, slightly moist. The invisible wall that kept adults safely apart had come down, and so fast it almost frightened her. She had not thought it could come down so easily. She waited for him to turn and cup her face, half-closed her eyes in readiness. And yet when he didn't, it wound through her in the matter-of-fact way of a dream that, of course, he would never take the lead. She would need to do that—just not now, with Nicholas strapped in below and her mothers' group expecting her.

"What do you think we should do with them?" she asked, because they were still staring at the drawings.

"I don't know," he said with a hint of his earlier reserve. "They're part of the house's history. If it were me, I guess I'd keep them."

"Maybe we'll do that," she said, and eased herself away.

THE OTHER MOTHERS WERE TRADING RENOVA-tion horror stories in Louise's family room, their little ones perched before them on the rug, heads bowed toward a bright mound of Baby Duplo. Louise had just finished redoing her kitchen, installing dark cherry cabinets and a granite-topped island that they'd all admired while pouring cream into their coffee cups. The contractor, however, had gone AWOL for two weeks, leaving her with no sink and not even a sheet of plywood for a counter. Rachel's en suite, meanwhile, desperately needed a facelift (it had one of those monstrous corner soaker tubs), but she didn't want to go with just anyone. Not after last time.

Everyone groaned, except for Tracey.

She was thinking about Alex. The way he'd looked at her when she eased herself away, what had almost happened, what she was pretty sure she could still make happen. Clasping her coffee cup, she gazed out past the babies to the patio with its bursting pots of red and white impatiens and imagined how she would slide her hands up his arms, intertwine her fingers behind his neck and draw his mouth to hers. Nicholas would be napping, of course. She squinted at the impatiens, blocking her child out of this picture. James needed to be blocked out as well. Remembering Sara in her cubicle next to his helped. But the key was to stay in that room. By focusing on the dustpan, the bucket, the drawings on the wall, she could keep Nicholas and James out long enough for Alex to caress her face, her waist, her breasts.

His touch was so real she almost moaned. She felt a sudden urge to say his name. "My painter, Alex, found something interesting on Friday."

"Oh, I didn't know you were having work done," Louise said.

Tracey explained then how they'd hired someone to redo the servant's room at the back of the house so they would have a proper guest room for her mother, how James had realized he just didn't have time to do the work himself (not mentioning the steak knife for obvious reasons). None of the other mothers had used this Alex before or even heard of him.

"Is he cute?" Rachel wanted to know. "Nothing like a little eye candy when you're stuck at home with a baby all day."

"Well, I think he could be fifty," Tracey said, hoping the heat rising to her face wasn't noticeable. "Anyway, the interesting thing is that when he was stripping the room, he found these two charcoal drawings on the plaster. A bust of a woman and one of a man, from when the house was first built in 1904. The woman looks like she might be the lady of the house." That stupid phrase again. "The man's really gorgeous. Alex thinks he looks like a rock star."

"Wow! Who drew them?" Nancy had glanced up from a guest towel she was embroidering with miniature daisies (she always had a DIY project on the go).

"Alex thinks a workman maybe."

"I wonder if they were lovers," Rachel said.

"I've been wondering that too," Tracey admitted.

"I bet they were," Rachel continued. "Except the lady was married so she could only meet him secretly. And then she tried to end things and he drew the pictures to expose her."

"Or maybe it was unrequited," Louise suggested. "He knew he couldn't have her, so he drew the portraits as a romantic gesture, knowing that she'd see them later. Funny that they didn't just paint over them instead of wallpapering, since you said it was a servant's room."

"That's what James thinks."

"So what are you going to do with these charcoal drawings on the wall?"

This was Ana. She was from Croatia or Armenia (Tracey could never remember which) and always seemed to be judging the rest of them. Once, when Louise was agonizing over ceramic or laminate flooring, Ana had noted grimly that in her country a woman might get one chance to remodel her kitchen, if she were very lucky.

"I don't know. Alex thinks we should keep them." Tracey wished she hadn't used his name again, especially after mentioning James. Her voice sounded airy and unconvincing.

"Oh, you should," Nancy enthused. "They'd make a wonderful focal point."

Louise suggested stencilling a border, something bold and leafy that would give the room a Tuscan feel. But Rachel had an even better idea. They could screw wooden picture frames around each drawing and get their painter to paint outside of these, Moroccan red maybe. Even Ana seemed to think this would be artistic.

"Oh, that sounds perfect," Tracey cried, feeling as if she'd wandered into a vast sunlit room where anything was possible. She was so grateful to these women for agreeing with Alex that they should keep the drawings.

Later, though, after she got home and stood staring at the lady and her workman lover on the fully stripped and wiped-down wall, she couldn't help wondering whether any of them would really do such a thing in her own dream house.

JAMES THOUGHT THE FRAME IDEA WAS RIDICULOUS.

"They're cool, Trace. But they're going to give your mom nightmares. And we won't be able to fit the bed." With his hand, he ruled off where the bottom of the man's frame would need to be screwed in. "Too low. See? We'll take photos, but we're going to have to get Alex to paint the whole room."

He was right. Her mother would hardly enjoy waking up to those blackened eyes staring down at her, even if they could make the bed fit. Moreover, repapering, which James halfheartedly suggested as a method to at least protect the drawings, was out of the question. Wallpaper, they agreed, was dated. What they wanted was a unified paint scheme leading from room to room. So Tracey fetched her paint chips and they taped the ones they liked beside the window for the best light, settling on a shade called Hawthorne Yellow she'd found in a Benjamin Moore brochure of historical colours. She was surprised by how happy she felt once this decision was made. Squinting at the tiny square of card stock, she pictured how restful the room would look when it was painted and had real pictures on the walls. After dinner, James took some photos with his new digital camera and commented that the woman was hot.

"So is the rock star," she teased back.

And since the evening was hot too, and Nicholas had fallen asleep earlier than expected, they brought a bottle of wine up to their room and had what they agreed in the morning was their best sex in years.

Tracey worried that Alex would be disappointed, disapproving even, but he only nodded in that sober way of his and drove off in the Volvo to buy the paint. After she put Nicholas down for his afternoon nap, she could hear the long, even strokes of a roller, broken up by the soft slap of a brush, but felt nervous interrupting him.

The day Alex returned for the second coat, Nicholas had a doctor's appointment and there were a few grocery items she needed to pick up, so she left the key under the mat again, still thinking she would see him later. And then what? It depended, she supposed, on where they were in the house. Whether Nicholas was napping. And after that? In a tiny corner of her mind, she could see herself driving away in the Volvo, Nicholas in his car seat in the back, and then a sunny apartment with simple but elegant furnishings, Alex's white coveralls hanging from a hook on the bedroom door. But she didn't have a chance to test any of this out because midway through the morning, he called the office to say the room was done, and James came home and paid him.

"He's certainly good value," James said at the time.

THEY NEVER HIRED HIM AGAIN. THERE WERE NO issues with his work. Five weeks later, however, Tracey discovered she was pregnant with Alice, and neither of them felt comfortable with a smoker in the house. When Rachel called the next spring looking for his number, Tracey had to explain they no longer had it.

The guest room unfortunately was just a little too small. When Tracey's mother came in September, they offered her Nicholas's room instead and shifted his crib into theirs. They never considered it for a baby room. It was too stuffy in summer, too cold in winter. Alice slept with them until she was old enough to share a bunk bed with her brother. So gradually the room filled up with old tax files, family photo albums, and baby equipment

they were finished with. Before moving to a more prac-
tical house in the same subdivision as Rachel and Louise,
they had a family room built on and got rid of the kitchen
stairs. The plan also had been to expand the upstairs
bathroom into what they now referred to as the junk
room, but after Sara transferred unexpectedly, selling the
Queen Anne for almost twice its purchase price, they
levelled with each other: they were not old-house people.

Naturally, they would always wish they'd taken more
before-and-after photos.

How many layers did I strip from that double parlour?
James would muse when they had another couple over
for dinner. Six or seven? Do you remember, hon?

WHAT SHE WOULD REMEMBER, AT LEAST FOR AS
long as they lived in that house, was standing in the
doorway after the room had first been done. How everything felt not just brighter but also tighter, as if the room
had in fact gone under a plastic surgeon's knife. Staring
at those four smooth walls, each now a delicate yellow,
Tracey had felt a lift as well. Even the view from the
window seemed brand-new, daylilies and purple cone-
flowers emerging reassuringly from what a few weeks
ago had been ominous clumps of leaves. She stroked
the thick coat of white on the sill, so fresh and clean
looking. Then pressed her face against the glass, sliding
her palms up the frame in a clumsy embrace. This, of
course, made her think of Alex. How could she not in
this room? And she almost shivered. She had not made

that mistake, not risked the future life she was creating with James, room by shining room. It amazed her, though, how close she'd come, and before leaving to collect a few things from the dryer, she made a point of tracing her fingers along the wall where the drawings had been, and where now there was only paint.

Orlando, 1974

MY FATHER SAYS STEPHEN ONLY THREW UP because of the Hawaiian pancakes and can still go to the Magic Kingdom. His throw-up has chunks of pineapple and this white goo that could be marshmallows or the Cool Whip. The white goo trembles on the pavement like a jellyfish.

"Don't look," my father says, hustling Dougie and me into the rental car.

"He's fine," he tells my mother, who's wiping Stephen's shirt with a Kleenex and doesn't look around.

In the backseat with my youngest brother, I think how things like this always happen to Stephen. If my father tosses a cigarette on the grass, Stephen is the one who steps on it and then has to wear a big cloth bandage on his foot. If the three of us are practising our jumps at the pool, he's the one who splits his chin open, bloodying not just the tiles on the edge but almost the whole deep end. Once when my mother was turning at the end of our street, he fell out of the car into the middle of all the traffic (he'd been playing with his door handle).

Turning out of the Pancake House parking lot, my father tells us it's a good thing that he threw up on the pavement and not in the rental car or at the Magic Kingdom. But my mother says Stephen might have caught a bug on the plane so my father is just going to have to drop the two of them off at Court of Flags.

Where we *should* be staying is the Contemporary Resort, which is on the Disney site. Not some budget motel an hour away. That's what she's said a few times since we got here. But my brothers and I love Court of Flags (the World Famous, my father reminds us, because that's what it says on the giant neon sign with all the flags). We love the long dim corridor with its smelly carpet squares, and the growling ice machine we race to with the bucket, and the jellybean-shaped pool with its black-and-white braided lounge chairs and view of dusty palms and the cars speeding by on International Drive.

My father keeps repeating that Stephen's fine. My mother tells him that he doesn't know what he's talking about and that she has no intention of trooping around an amusement park with a sick child. Stephen doesn't say a word, so maybe he really did catch a bug on the plane. Or maybe he's just happy to be the one sitting on my mother's lap for a change, instead of Dougie. When my father slows in front of the motel and I see those tiny flags from all the countries of the world rattling in the wind, I don't want to have to troop around the Magic Kingdom all day either. I want to keep practising my front crawl while my mother reads her book on a lounge chair, like yesterday. But I'm stuck in the back with Dougie and can only watch as she tugs on the big glass door, then vanishes inside with Stephen

Once we're walking down Main Street U.S.A., though, I forget all about my mother and the pool at Court of Flags. In the distance, I can see Cinderella's castle shimmering in the sun like a giant birthday cake. The buildings on either side of us remind me of cakes too, with fancy curlicues of white icing decorating their doors and windows. A horse-drawn streetcar weaves through the crowd of visitors, and then a fire truck and a marching band, and Sleepy and Dopey from the Seven Dwarfs, and Winnie the Pooh with the honey pot stuck to his head like a fluffy beige top hat. Dougie and I keep calling to my father to look, and he teases us that our mouths are even bigger than our Hawaiian pancakes.

With my new 110 camera, I take a picture of a man in a striped blazer like in *Mary Poppins* holding out a bouquet of Mickey Mouse balloons, and one of Dougie standing beside an overflowing flower cart, and another of my father grinning from the stocks.

But Dougie gets tired of looking at old-fashioned buildings. He wants to ride the train to Adventureland and tries to drag my father by the arm.

My father just laughs. "We have the whole day," he says. "We can do anything we want. But maybe we should save a few rides for when Stephen and Mommy come."

We save the swan boats and the giant teacups and the Hall of Presidents and 20,000 Leagues Under the Sea. I feel a little bad saving the Hall of Presidents, since it looks so boring. On the Jungle River Cruise, I start to feel bad too, because Stephen's favourite TV show is *Mutual of Omaha's Wild Kingdom*.

When a crocodile opens its mouth right next to our boat, Dougie grabs my father's arm again. "Is it real?" he cries.

"It sure is," my father says, and hugs him close.

Between rides, he buys us ice cream cones and bags of caramel corn and in the Frontier Trading Post lets us pick out any souvenir we want. Dougie picks a dark brown cowboy hat, and my father picks out a tan one from the same pile for Stephen. I pick a Hawaiian doll the size of my hand. She has a grass skirt and shiny black hair with a red flower in it and huge teardrop eyes spaced far apart. I love her hard plastic face and the way all her fingers except the thumb stick together like a fin.

In the rental car, I name her Red Flower.

When we get back to Court of Flags, Stephen and my mother are sitting on the bed that she and I sleep in. The curtains are closed because Stephen's watching *Truth or Consequences*. He's got on his striped corduroy pants from the plane and a striped T-shirt. The stripes go in different directions, so he must have dressed himself after the Pancake House. My mother has on her pink terry-cloth coverup with the zipper and I can see a strap from her two-piece bathing suit. She's leaning up against the headboard on the side closest to her night table. A glass with a little Orange Crush in it sits beside the phone, which is yellow like her one at home. After school sometimes, she goes into her bedroom and whispers into this phone's small mouthpiece until I knock to say our show is over. She's always in a good mood afterward, letting us eat our dinner on the TV trays and, when my father comes in the door, pouring him a drink from one of the bottles in the cupboard above the kitchen sink and asking about his day.

Right now, she's asking about our day at the Magic Kingdom.

"There were real crocodiles," Dougie says. "And a whole family of elephants having a water fight. And Daddy bought me a cowboy hat."

My father slides the second hat toward Stephen on the bed. He touches the brim but doesn't look around. On the TV, Bob Barker is laughing at a man trying to ride a unicycle. The studio audience is laughing too, hard like rain.

"See my new doll," I say, but I know my mother thinks I'm too old for dolls.

Next to the TV is a big mirror and when I lean far enough forward, I can see all five of us in it. I hold Red Flower up to my cheek and notice for the first time how small and close together my eyes are. I'm not pretty, not the way she is, or my mother.

"And what did you two do all day?" my father asks, and in the mirror, I see him glance at the night table with its nearly empty glass and yellow phone.

"I had French fries," Stephen says.

And Dougie goes, "Awww, no fair, I want French fries."

TODAY, INSTEAD OF DRIVING ALL THAT WAY TO the pancake restaurant that made Stephen throw up, we simply walk down the corridor to the motel coffee shop. My mother orders Stephen, Dougie, and me little boxes of Rice Krispies, which she carves open with her butter knife, along with tall glasses of thick, bubbly homogenized milk that tastes like vanilla milkshake, and coffee and toast for herself and my father. While we're waiting for the bill, he lights a cigarette. He smokes another in the rental car, flinging the butt at the line in the centre of the highway that races beside us all the way to the Magic Kingdom.

The walk from the parking lot to Main Street U.S.A. takes a lot longer this time. There are all these people in our way.

"Because it's a Saturday," my father says.

I wrap the strap of my camera around one wrist and cradle Red Flower in my other arm. When the Contemporary Resort's monorail zooms overhead, I hold her extra close.

"See the Mickey Mouse in the flowers," I say to Stephen, but he's poking Dougie in the shoulder, pretending his finger is a gun.

They're both wearing their new cowboy hats with matching shorts-and-shirt sets, Stephen's blue and Dougie's brown. I have on the denim hot-pants overalls and blue-checked blouse my mother put out for me on the motel chair. She's wearing a green halter dress I haven't seen before. Her sunglasses are the white ones with the huge dark lenses that always make me feel as if she's floated off somewhere—like the mother in that poem,

ORLANDO, 1974

the one who goes down to the end of the town in her golden gown and is never seen again. Once, after my swimming lesson, I thought she really was gone and couldn't stop crying, even when I saw her coming across the deck in her pink coverup.

I always worry now where she is when I'm at school. I don't about my father. I know he's in his office, filling up the brown glass ashtray on his desk with butts, mumbling into his Dictaphone. He looks shorter today, fatter too, especially on Main Street when Honest John creeps up behind him. This is just a man in a fox costume, I know that. But, close up, Honest John's rubber eyes and the clumps of matted orange fur on his giant head scare me, the way the drunks downtown do when my mother leaves us in the car too long.

On the train to Adventureland, the sky goes the same soot grey as the palms at Court of Flags. The lineup for the Jungle River Cruise takes much longer this time, and the ride itself is not as much fun. Even Dougie can tell how fake those elephants look sitting on their bums in the muddy water. I take a picture of them anyway, and one of my mother in her white sunglasses, and one of my father pointing excitedly at a crocodile's spying eyes.

He's in the lineup at the Outpost Canteen when I notice Red Flower is gone.

"Don't get hysterical," my mother says.

"She could be anywhere," my father says when he gets back, staring at my mother. He promises to buy me a new doll at the Trading Post, but I don't want a new doll. I want Red Flower.

"Don't be so spoiled," my mother says.

And my father says, "It's just a doll."

But everything inside me is spinning, and I can't stop this spinning, any more than I could stop our giant tea-cup, which the second it began to tilt, I wanted to get off. My brothers in their cowboy hats stretch their legs out on the curb. They bite into their hot dogs and watch me get hysterical.

The lineup for 20,000 Leagues Under the Sea is the longest of all. Stephen squats on the pavement and scoops dirt into his cowboy hat. Dougie copies him, even though my mother tells him not to. When they flip the hats over, tiny mushroom clouds of dust fly up.

"It won't be long now," my father says.

But he's wrong, and when we finally board Captain Nemo's submarine, I can't help noticing how the sea-weed and the rocks and even the giant squid are made of the same thick rubber as Honest John's head. Stuck to the underside of the porthole window is a fresh wad of gum. It's the same yucky white as the marshmallow goo.

"Well, that certainly wasn't worth the wait," my mother says.

And I feel bad for my father, because this whole trip was his idea. Then I remember Red Flower and how he sided with my mother, how he always spanks us when she tells him to.

"Red Flower will find a nice new family," he says when we're back on Main Street, but I won't look at him and drag my sneaker toes so I don't have to walk beside him either.

ORLANDO, 1974

Stephen and Dougie have run ahead and are cocking their fingers at each other through the crowd. "Bam. Bam-bam. Bam-bam-bam."

Only my mother now is near me. Her lips under the white sunglasses twitch as if she's thinking about something funny. I let a fat woman in a floppy straw hat come between us, then a whole family holding out bright pink plumes of cotton candy, so that she'll think I'm gone, so she'll be the one to get hysterical. But only my father looks around.

He waves to me and calls to my brothers to come back, then stops by the man in the striped blazer and picks out three Mickey Mouse balloons. Green for Stephen, orange for Dougie, and red for me.

"Hold on tight," he says, and I clench the string so hard my whole palm aches as though someone's bit it.

The Magic Kingdom parking lot is just one huge traffic jam.

"This is why we should have stayed at the Contemporary," my mother says when we're sitting in the rental car.

"As you've made abundantly clear," my father snaps, and she gazes out her window as if she wishes she could speed away from him by monorail.

Dougie and I hold our balloons on our laps, rubbing their dusty ears and their flat eyes and noses. Stephen lets his float out his window. He wraps the string around the door handle, then sticks his head out to see how far up it goes.

All around us are other families in stuck cars. Fathers resting elbows on cranked-down windows, the smoke from their cigarettes clouding over steering wheels. Mothers, rigid beside them, their hair half-hidden in flowered scarves or falling out of sprayed-tight curls. The kids in these cars stare mostly straight ahead at the tan or turquoise or cherry-red backs of their parents' seats. Some are wearing Mickey Mouse ears or little cloth caps with Magic Kingdom printed on them, others cowboy hats or Indian-brave feathers. In a station wagon in the next row, a curly-haired toddler presses her mouth against the glass and blows us a smudgy flower kiss before her sister pulls her down. Nothing else stirs—the only sound apart from the motors a faint ringing from the telephone towers that line the parking lot like metal Christmas trees.

Suddenly, the car in front of ours jolts forward. Now ours does too. Dougie looks at me, his face as white as Cool Whip, and throws up all over my bare legs and Mickey Mouse balloon. And I can't stop myself. The feeling rises, fills up my throat and mouth, hot and stale like the air inside the submarine, like the smell of my father's squashed butts in the ashtray of the tan armrest between him and my mother. I turn to Stephen, and even before I throw up too, the string has started to unravel, the green balloon slipping out of our reach, above the car roofs and the telephone towers and all the corners of the Magic Kingdom.

ORLANDO, 1974

Bear Country

WHEN HIS SON DESCENDS AROUND NOON, RAY IS still a little high.

"Well, look who's joined the living!" he says, and considers making a lame dad joke about watching the sunrise together. Except he can already tell by the way Gabe's climbing down the ladder that this is going to be one of their bad days.

Gabe jabs a heel out behind him, misses the floor, jabs again. "When are you going to get them?"

All he has on are the black sweatpants he's been wearing day and night, though for once he isn't clutching the laptop. Without it, his chest looks unnaturally pale, mushroom-like, puffing out of the waistband of the sweatpants. He's gained more weight since Ray moved out, has love handles now.

"Whoa!" Ray raises his hands as if he's just been busted, which is how he mostly feels. "What about a

'Good afternoon, Dad'? 'What exciting adventures have you got in store for us today?'"

"You said you'd do it."

"I said what?"

"That you'd get them. Yesterday. You said."

Christ, he might have.

Yesterday had been one of their good days. Gabe came down before nine for a change, just as Ray was rolling the first of the two joints he's been allowing himself up here. The night one, which he smokes spread-eagled in his full glory on the bed he used to share with Gwyneth, is a symbol of his new freedom. This morning one is more contemplative. He smokes it usually on the deck steps, gazing out over their scorched yard to the river and thinking about his future. This summer marks the first time in thirty years he hasn't been entangled with some woman, and he intends to keep it that way. Stick to the path, no more diversions. That's what he tells himself at any rate when he's smoking weed in the dewy early stillness, his son overhead sleeping or doing God knows what on the laptop, and the rest of his life unfolding like a roadmap.

Yesterday, however, Gabe came down before Ray could breathe in that first heady taste of possibility, so he set the joint aside and made a big pot of coffee and his special pancakes with the last of the wizened blueberries. He even convinced Gabe to put down the computer and go out with him in the green canoe that came with the cottage and that Ray spent a whole summer sanding and varnishing. And when they pulled up at their old picnic spot, a granite ledge that Jenna at four or five nicknamed Solid Rock, he spread out the batik tablecloth, the Tupperware containers filled with trail mix and cut-up melon, just as Gwyn used to do.

"Can't this wait till we get back to civilization?" he asks.

Gabe grabs a fistful of his hair, which is patchy like an old man's because he's pulled so much out. "You lied. All you do is lie."

"I didn't lie. I don't lie. It's just I think you might find them cheaper in the city."

"No, you're a liar. All you do is lie, lie, lie."

Ray grabs his own thinning hair.

Gwyn knows how to handle Gabe when he gets like this, but Ray's still adjusting. A poor excuse, he's aware, given it's been four years since Gabe first pulled out all his eyelashes and two since OCD and agoraphobia got added to his original diagnosis. Mind you, Ray was already mostly gone by then, so wrapped up in Angie that the kids, his job, Gwyneth were like an all-day news channel warning of disaster from another room.

Gabe is padding between the ladder and the kitchen table. "Just one pack." He claws his cheeks. "Please, Dad."

Christ, what's he want with Pokémon now?

It was Gwyneth who got them into all that madness, surprising Gabe in grade two with a base set and a binder, spending hours listening to him describe each creature's special power. She must have hoped the cards would help him fit in better. As if there was ever any chance of that. The kid might as well have belonged to another species. His kid. Sometimes, during morning drop-off, Ray could hardly bear to watch Gabe shuffle into the maw of that elementary school where on a good day no one stole his cards or pulled his pants down, his frame as delicate as a bird's before the Zoloft bulked him out.

He's wishing now that he'd had the sense to shove those old cards of Gabe's into one of his garbage bags with the other junk. The stack was wedged behind several rusted paint cans at the back of the shed, which Ray's been cleaning out on Gwyneth's orders so they can list the cottage at the end of the summer. Some of the individual cards a little water-damaged, yet their stats basically readable. Well, look what I found, he announced when he came in for a beer, tossing the stack on his son's lap where it clanked against the keyboard. But he should have known by the fevered way Gabe grabbed it, thumbing off the elastic bands, moving his lips along the cards' weathered edges. He wasn't up there all night watching porn. He was checking out nineties cartoons, roaming collectors' forums, salivating over holographic Pikachus.

Ray wants to tell him that none of this will matter later. That he's a great kid with a great future, that he loves him. But also to grow up, go back to school, find a girl, or a boy if that's what he prefers. Get his act together.

Instead, he caves on the cards. "Okay, okay, look, I'll bike to the store and see if I can get a pack there. But you've gotta calm down, Gabe." He senses the kid's flinch before his fingers even get that close. "And go outside, okay, pal? Go for a swim."

WHEELING HIS OLD RALEIGH TEN-SPEED OUT OF the shed, Ray thinks again about his love. When does he not? When he's sleeping, he supposes. Ah, but then he dreams about her. Teasing, tormenting dreams in which Angie pretends to want him back only to resurface with some other guy. Just a friend. She shrugs. As if she thinks Ray won't notice how she's stroking this new friend's hairy forearm. Still, he's better than he was six months ago. No longer waking up in his clothes, mouth clotted with the oblivion of the night before, not freaking out colleagues and distant friends with drunken statuses on Facebook. And now that he's pedalling up the driveway with his empty knapsack limp against his back and the buzz from the joint dulling all pain, he feels almost his old self again.

An hour north by car is an industrial park with all the usual soulless big-box stores, but when he isn't out of liquor, Ray much prefers this forty-five-minute ride to the bait-and-variety store at the highway turnoff. For the first few kilometres, the road follows the contour of the river, past wooden posts cluttered with handmade signs, the family names and their apostrophe errors (*Fisher's*, *The Carroll's*) gouged or burnt into them. Usually, he would have to keep glancing over his shoulder for cars. Today, though, the road's deserted. The heat most likely. Everyone sticking close to home, enjoying the river's cool depths where Ray has occasionally glimpsed huge, dark, primeval-looking fish. Or twirling about on the sunlit surface in inflated swans and hippos—a thought that only adds to the rush as he swoops inland on the Raleigh and the river and its cottages drop away behind him like ash from a cigarette.

Up ahead, he can see the old forest-fire-danger sign, its faded arrow hovering close to red. No rain for six weeks and a fire ban for four. Why he hasn't finished cleaning out the shed, not that Gwyneth can get her head around this. She wants him to drive all their scrap wood and other junk to the dump, when what he wants is to wait until the ban is lifted and build a bonfire on the beach. Toast marshmallows with Gabe. Dance around the funeral pyre. I thought you cared about landfill, he countered the last time she got him on his cell. I do, she fired back, but I also care about people with asthma and not starting forest fires.

Ray takes a cleansing breath and pictures, as he's done a few times already this summer, a beautiful woman sitting cross-legged on the grassy shoulder of the road. Wavy dark hair to her waist. A long sheer summer dress that reveals the soft roundedness of her breasts. Something in her lap: a bowl of fresh-picked blueberries or a bouquet of wildflowers.

Hey, he imagines her call out to him. Where are you going?

Of course, his luck, he'll meet a bear.

That happened once, the last time he and Gwyn and the kids all came up together. He'd volunteered to bike to the store, for a carton of milk or a loaf of bread but really so he could talk to Angie on his cell without Jenna or Gabe busting in on him. The bear was standing on its hind legs before he even noticed it. An adult male, a good six feet tall, staring at him from the middle of the road no more than fifty metres away. He couldn't think of anything to do—too late to make a wide berth and no bell on the Raleigh—so just kept cycling, as he would tell the kids, straight into the jaws of death. Only then, just as he got close enough that he could make out the white hairs in its fur, an old blue pickup appeared and the bear dropped to all fours, scrambling into the ditch like a spooked dog. My angel was watching out for me, he teased when he got Angie on the line.

Gliding over the spot, Ray shifts into higher gear, hoping to recapture some of that same euphoria, how he seemed to be riding not a beat-up ten-speed but a monstrous cresting wave. Instead, he notices an uneasy silence on the road. Not only no cars, no signs of life of any kind, not even a small bird swooping through the undergrowth. No cross-legged woman either. Still, he can't stop checking both the shoulders, he's not sure why.

THE BAIT-AND-VARIETY STORE DOESN'T CARRY Pokémon cards. Maybe it never did. The teenaged girl at the cash stared at him as if he'd asked for a roll of film or a beaver hat, so Ray has spent the past ten minutes examining the toy aisle where he bought Jenna and Gabe so many of the plastic sand buckets he's found in the shed but that nowadays seems to carry only candy-filled space guns and grabbers and other overpriced junk. One of the grabbers is shaped like a shark's jaws.

There's also a box of these plastic turds that remind him of soft-serve sundaes but with white eyes and surprised red lips. *Pooplets*, the box says.

The girl is staring again, more suspiciously now, as if she expects him to try to sneak out with a Pooplet underneath his shirt. Christ, what is it about him?

Ray drifts to the back of the store where the bait and other fishing gear are kept. He hasn't fished in years, but he's noticed his old rod is still in the shed. Maybe Gabe would like to try it out. He knows Gabe won't but can't help handling each of the smooth metal fish on a giant pegboard display of lures. Then, possibly because he's already feeling accused, he plucks off an iridescent silver-green one and hides it in his fist. On his way to the cash, he grabs a bag of soft brown bread and a jar of roasted peanuts, making a show of plunking them down all innocent on the counter. He's not sure he really means to steal the lure but likes how the idea has begun sharpening his brain. Then pulling a ten out of his jeans pocket, he drops it.

A woman behind him in line stoops and picks it up for him. "Going fishing?"

She's kind of cute, about his age. "Yes, ma'am. Wanna come?"

And to his surprise she plays along. "Love to. Wait for me outside?"

Ray grins at her and tosses the tiny metal fish onto the counter. "Okay, but I only have one rod."

"I guess we'll have to share then."

She's smiling at him in a way that suggests this might not be just banter, but he could be mistaken, and now the girl is shoving a plastic bag at him.

"Thanks, I have this," he says, sliding the bread and peanuts and the lure into his knapsack. "See ya out there then," he says to the woman, though he can't tell if she hears.

ON THE STORE'S PORCH, RAY STUDIES THE COM-munity noticeboard. It's as beat-up as the fire-danger sign yet as usual papered over in fresh warnings—about the fire ban, safe boating, proper garbage disposal, a proposed dam project 100K away that could affect water levels. One notice features a silhouette of a bear's head. *An adult black bear has been spotted in this area*, it says. *Please use caution when walking and be aware of your sur-roundings. Fish and Wildlife has been notified.* Ray grins, thinking how thankful the fish must have been for the heads-up, then glances over his shoulder.

The woman still hasn't come out. He doesn't want to look as if he's waiting for her, so he steps off the porch and strolls past the half dozen or so parked cars to the old Chip Wagon, where he used to take the kids sometimes without telling Gwyneth. He parks himself on top of a picnic table with his back to the highway, twists open the lid of the peanuts and pours himself a handful, wishing he'd thought to also buy a pop or a bottled water, yet feeling too lazy, or something, to try the Chip Wagon.

It's under new management this summer. The sign has been re-lettered. He's pleased to see this still lists *pogo's & o rings*, just as he's always pleased to see the misplaced apostrophes on his neighbours' cottage signs. Beside the takeout window is a barrel of geraniums and on top of the garbage bin one of those hard plastic owls to ward off predators, at least the feathered kind. Gwyneth called him a predator once. She went a little crazy on him near the end. Well, to be fair, he went a little crazy too. And again after Angie left. Almost lost his job. Almost got himself killed, weaving through four lanes of traffic with his bottle of Jack Daniel's.

A van door slides open, but it's not that woman from the store making a hasty getaway. It's two little kids, a girl and a boy about the ages of Jenna and Gabe when he used to buy them o rings on the sly. They race each other to the takeout window while Mom and Dad take their time extricating themselves from bucket seats. The van's a new Dodge Caravan, fire-engine red, with a couple of two-seater kayaks strapped to the roof and a tangle of bikes protruding over the bumper. Ray watches as Dad tests all the straps and Mom reaches inside for a bright yellow knapsack and her children's sunhats. He doesn't recognize them, but then he barely knows anyone up here anymore. All new families, just starting out, amassing all the protective gear, hoping cars and bikes and fancy boats will keep them safe.

Behind him comes a blast of dry air from a passing tractor-trailer. Another, from one going in the opposite direction, lifts his shirt. On the drive north with Gabe, he felt as if he'd taken a wrong turn somewhere and they were heading into the African savanna. The roadside grasses, even the evergreens sunbaked, sepia-toned. Global warming, they called it once. Bring it on, he used to joke. Not anymore. From the picnic table, the only flora he can see not coated in highway dust are the Chip Wagon's geraniums, which are so pink and wet-looking it occurs to him they might be plastic; the only fauna a gull that, undeterred by the scare-owl, glides to the ground to snatch a fallen fry. That woman must have driven off after all. He imagines her smiling to herself as she turns the key in the ignition, or her husband does, and hops down to fetch his bike, in a way relieved.

ON THE RIDE HOME, THOUGH, HE SPOTS HER, walking up his side of the road with a slack cloth bag. From the back, she looks younger than in the store, yet when she turns, he can make out flecks of grey in her thick shoulder-length brown hair and tiny lines at the corners of her mouth and wide-spaced eyes. Still, definitely kind of cute, in her snug jeans and grey T-shirt with a faded print in black of what looks like a slanting row of firs.

"Well, hello," she says when he stops. "If it isn't the fisherman."

"Hello, yourself."

She looks right at him then and says, "Where are you going?" And his heart pounds, because that's what his cross-legged woman always says.

"Home," he tells her, then corrects himself. "Cottage."

"Up here with your family?"

"Not exactly." They're walking together now, nice and slow, only the Raleigh between them. Ray observes her glance at the hairs on his forearm, feels the hairs tingle in response.

"Wife and kids coming up later?" she asks.

"Nope, divorced. Divorcing actually. It's just my boy and me."

"And you've left him alone?"

"He's fifteen. I think he can manage."

"Okay, I guess you're off the hook. Just the one?"

"No, two. But my daughter, she's not that thrilled with me these days."

"So I'm guessing it's your fault you're divorcing?"

"You ask a lot of questions," Ray says.

"Yeah, people tell me that."

He knows he doesn't have to say why his marriage is breaking up, then does anyway. "Okay, so, yeah, I fell in love with someone else."

"Oh," she says with a wry smile. "I see."

Again, he could keep his mouth shut, let her assume he's taken. Instead, he hears himself say he's not with this person anymore. "Not that that makes any difference to my wife. Probably for the best. I'm not that good at being married."

"Me too," she confides. "I'm not much of a marriage person either."

He gives a low whistle, to suggest not just surprise but also arch approval, then glances down at her bag. "So what you got in there?"

The woman pulls out a single dimpled lemon. "I'm staying with my sister and her husband. They own a place"—she points vaguely—"over that direction. It's kind of tense. My brother-in-law is a total prick. I go on a lot of errands to the store just to get out of there."

"You should be careful walking on your own," he warns with mock gallantry. "This is bear country after all."

And he's just about to tell the story of his close call on this same stretch of the road, how he kept on cycling into the jaws of death, when she announces, "I'm not afraid of bears. Not the black ones. I feel sorry for them."

"What about when they treat your garbage like a fast-food joint?" he says, thinking of a morning some years ago when a whole family got into theirs.

"It's called food conditioning," the woman informs him. "Bears are very smart and adaptable. They only need to eat garbage once to develop a taste for it. And you're right to call it fast food. They get addicted to the ease and convenience of human garbage and then they grow less wild, more dependent on us. And what do we do? We murder them."

The faded image on her shirt he realizes too late is an arty rendering of a bear walking, the slanted treetops meant to represent its furry back.

"Cubs are especially vulnerable." The woman continues sternly, as if she's seen those grainy early-morning photos Gwyn took through the sliding door. The mama nosing the garbage lid toward the river, her two babies pawing through burst kitchen catchers, licking yogurt pods on the dewed grass. Ray's own babies' faces pressed against the glass. "And not just because they're eating garbage. They're also getting orphaned at enormous rates because of clear-cutting and forest fires. Sometimes, their mothers can't produce any milk for them. They're too stressed." Ray peers ahead hoping for the river to show up, but suddenly she drops the lecture. "So what are you going to do next, Mr Fisherman? Now that you're divorc*ing*?"

"I don't know yet. My wife wants to sell the cottage. If we get a good price, I might quit my job, buy a used van, travel down the coast."

"Really? That's one of my dreams too. I saw this ad on Craigslist for a VW bus, great condition, just twenty-five hundred."

Now it's Ray's turn to enthuse. "That's a good price. I bought an old bus once for five hundred. I thought I could fix it up, but it drove my wife crazy sitting on the driveway, so I had to get rid of it."

"Sounds like your wife makes a lot of decisions."

He bristles again. She's pretty mouthy. What he says, though, is, "I'm trying to be a better fisherman and not cast aspersions."

"You're funny, you know."

He grins, though he isn't feeling funny and hasn't for quite awhile. "Yeah. People tell me that."

They've stopped walking. Behind her, the shoulder slopes into a well of browning ferns and charred cattails. On the other side of the ditch, a slim path leads up into the woods. The woman is still talking. She's telling him more about her prick brother-in-law, how he's always coming on to her. How she's divorced herself, but thankfully no kids. How she too feels at a crossroads in her life. But Ray's not listening that closely. He's thinking about that path and how much cooler it must feel under its canopy of firs. Also about his own path, whether he should buy himself a van, maybe that vw bus on Craigslist. Or build a cabin in the woods, go off-grid where no one can find him unless he wants them to.

Then he hears her say, "I hate that it's so hard these days to meet anyone except online. I just can't go there. I need to talk to a person in the flesh before I feel any kind of real connection. You know what I mean?"

She's looking right at him again, and he feels himself get slightly hard. "Yeah."

He half expects her to reach across the bike and stroke his arm, the way in his dreams Angie strokes the arms of her new friends. Instead, she twists her lips into another of the wry smiles he's starting to realize are more like grimaces.

"Want to walk the rest of the way with me? My sister would love you." For a second, Ray wonders if she's suggesting a threesome, only then she adds, "It would totally piss off my brother-in-law if I showed up with you."

"I'm not sure I want to mess with some guy I've never met," he says.

"I'm just kidding. He won't care. He probably won't even be there. Seriously, come. We've got lots of beer. And it's sooo hot. It must be thirty-eight degrees. What else are you going to do today, Mr Fisherman?" And this time she does reach across the bike and gently touches the hairs on the back of his hand.

As soon as they start walking, though, Ray can feel it, not just the heat of her body swaying closer now to his but her almost imperceptible need, like a light, sticky web he's stumbled into by accident. He pictures the scene lying in wait for him. The long hot dock with its 220 hp jet boat (twin inboard engines, leather seats), canoe and paddleboat, a semicircle of brightly coloured Adirondack chairs discreetly chained together. The sister, an older, softer version of the woman at his side, handing him a beer in its moist foam sleeve. The two of them vying for his attention. A tight hug or something more with one of them when the other's gone, and the brother-in-law—also gone, but where and for how long?

They've reached the bend in the road and the woman is swerving to the left and he's swerving with her, conscious of a sign in the shape of a lobster at the end of a driveway, an ash tree wreathed in faded prayer flags. He's gripping the handlebars tighter than he needs to, and the jar of peanuts in the knapsack keeps jabbing his spine. Then he remembers. He's a free man now, unfettered and alive as the old song goes, and to prove this, he stops in his tracks.

"Look, babe, I'm not sure I'm quite ready to meet the folks yet."

"Oh, come, please come. You need a cold beer. I sure do." She tugs at the neckline of her shirt, flapping the V-shaped sweat stain between her breasts.

"Thanks, but I don't think I will. Not today."

"Tomorrow then? I didn't mean all that crap about my brother-in-law. He's fine. Really. Or we could just go for another walk. Meet right here? Tomorrow, say two o'clock?"

"Yeah, sure."

The woman touches the back of his hand again. Then she trails her fingers up his forearm, and he lowers his face to meet hers.

"Whoa," he murmurs, though he's not particularly surprised, either by the kiss or the chapped urgency of her parted lips.

"Be here," she says with a little pout.

RAY'S STILL GRINNING AS HE SHOULDERS THE screen door ajar. He pries off his shoes, drops the knapsack on the kitchen table, opens the fridge, then a can of beer, loudly, with bravado, so that Gabe knows he's back. But the kid must still be sleeping or so deep in cybernation that even a tsunami wouldn't stir him. The silence comes as a reprieve. Not that Ray's all that worried about the Pokémon cards. He's sure he can ride over his son's hysterics, not get dragged down this time—in part because of the woman from the store, the way she looked at him and the way he felt when he disappointed her, the lovely possibilities that lie ahead. Only the longer he stands with his beer, staring at the white IKEA table he assembled for Gwyneth in this very spot ten years ago, the more his head feels back in a vise.

And now his cell is pinging from the couch. If Jenna were here, she'd roll her eyes. What's the point of owning one, Dad, if you're never going to have it with you? But the phone reminds him too much of Angie, especially all those texts he sent her after. Not to mention the times before, when Gwyn would call, usually about Gabe, and he'd be with his love, and she'd know it, and her voice would harden, or just sound tired.

Today, he has three unread messages, all from Gwyneth.
Just checking in about the shed ☺
How's Gabe?? ☺ ☺

And the one that just came in: *Don't forget the realtor's coming Tuesday!!!!* ☺ ☺ ☺

He's not sure he even wants to sell. What about the kids, he asked when she last brought up the realtor. Shouldn't we think about them? And she made that little breathy sound on the line, like she can't believe she married such a moron. And now he can't help picturing her new guy beside her as she texts (*Sorry, hon, I've just got to send my ex his chores*), which reminds him of that woman insinuating how his wife makes all his decisions for him—when it was so bloody obvious, despite her free and easy manner, that she only wanted to start making them herself.

He places his wife's smiley faces face-down on the table, swallows the rest of the beer, unpacks the bread and peanuts. The lure he lays on his palm. Maybe Gabe would like it. A peace offering until he can find a way to get the cards. He closes his fist around the little silver-green fish, gently so as not to puncture himself, and climbs partway up the ladder. It's the first time this summer he's done this, and he's struck by how cramped and airless the loft is. He needs to tell the kid to crack open a window. But Gabe's not there. Ray stares at the duffle bag collapsed under the eaves like roadkill, the futon with its single dark purple sheet, and the grubby laptop covered in stickers. What happened to the spool beds and the wicker dress-up chest? Purged during one of Gwyneth's spring visits, he supposes, along with the blue dish cabinet she's claimed is from her side, all the photos off the fridge. As he climbs back down, he can hear her in his head. You left him alone, all afternoon? But Gabe won't even swim. Yesterday, he just watched Ray from the rock. And he wouldn't hurt himself, which is the fear he knows that stalks Gwyneth and why she called his cell all those times he was with Angie. But the thought pricks at him.

Also pricking him is the fishing lure. He tugs the hook out of his palm and, when it appears, rubs the bead of blood with the heel of his other hand, then drops the metal fish onto the table with the phone and yanks open the sliding door. The deck's surface is deceptively hot, like a bed of embers, and he can only hop from one board to another until he thinks to grab his towel from the rail and drops it under his feet. Across the river, he can just make out above the tree line a hazy coin of sun. It's later than he realized. Shadows gathering along the beach. Tomorrow he'll take Gabe fishing. Or maybe they'll drive together to the industrial park as they should have done today. Find those bleeding Pokémon cards. Stop at the Chip Wagon on the way back for o rings. He doesn't feel good making that woman wait on the road for nothing, but he also knows how these things play out. That if he wants, he can run into her again.

He's so focused on working all this through that he doesn't notice the junk from the shed. When he does, he yells at the river. "Fuck!"

All his garbage bags have been ripped open. Rusted paint cans and ruined brushes lie strewn about the yard along with bleached sand buckets and cracked shovels, the disintegrating boxes of family board games, their remaining cardboard chits and counters and coins and cards, their tokens and dice and miniature figurines, glinting in the late-afternoon light. Bears is his first thought. But the shed door has been unlatched, the youth-sized life jackets he'd set aside to sell through the community noticeboard tossed helter-skelter across the blueberry bushes, his old rod flung into a sprawling nest of fishing line. And what bear could do that?

Christ, where was Gabe when all this was going on?

Then he spots him.

His son is crouched in the lee of the shed, the black sweatpants and a thin grey hoodie camouflaging him against the coming darkness. He's hunting for some-thing, piecing through the scrap wood, moving his hands blindly over the bits of garbage on the withered grass. Suddenly, he rocks back on his heels and with a strangled sound, not wholly sob or howl, grabs a hunk of his own hair.

If there were someplace left on this ravaged earth where Ray could think to run, he would.

Hyacinth Girl

THE POT OF FLOWERS WAS SITTING—WAITING for her, it would later seem—on the table in Daniel's shoe-filled hall. Oh, she thought with a quiver of surprise, someone's dropped these off for his birthday. They were hyacinths, the large Dutch variety. Not Laura's favourite: too showy, their heavy heads too quick to topple over. Yet the three upright flowers, two dark purple, one blue, seemed a cheerful sign of spring and she was in a mood to be cheerful.

She could hear the shower going down the hall. Daniel had texted to say he'd gotten back late from his run so to let herself in with the key under the milk crate. She'd been walking briskly from her car, worried she might be late herself, when the phone vibrated in her coat pocket, and slipping her hand around it, she'd felt a quiet happiness, knowing the message would be from her son, and then amusement at the milk crate. As a student in Toronto in the eighties, she'd scavenged milk crates too, to store her books and modest record collection, and she remembered feeling inordinately proud of a rare scratched-up yellow one she'd stolen from an alley behind a goulash restaurant near Queen and Bathurst. You should have kept it, Daniel had groaned when she told him, just as he had about the Olympia electric typewriter she'd written all her essays on.

The shower noise cut out and he emerged from the bathroom. Steam billowing into the hall, a thin olive-green towel tucked around his hips. He'd always been tall for his age, but since starting university, his shoulders had broadened and his waist begun to appear more tapered, giving him a gangly, big-boned elegance. His father, Mike, was shorter and had a stockier build, especially now that he'd developed gout in one foot and apparently couldn't exercise. Daniel, to Laura's pleasure, resembled the men on her side now more.

"Hey," he said, flipping back his hair, which he'd recently started growing out.

"Happy birthday!" Laura held up a small gift bag by its raffia handle.

Daniel grinned. "Just give me a sec."

The cramped third-floor walk-up that he shared with two other English students was stuffy, especially with the bathroom door open. She rested the gift bag next to the hyacinths to undo her scarf, then examined them more closely. They weren't store-bought. The pot was terra cotta rather than the usual plastic or cheap ceramic and its wide green bow real silk, while the flowers themselves appeared to have bloomed that very morning and were so lush, so exquisite that even the table, a rickety IKEA one Daniel had found on the sidewalk, seemed transfigured. Laura felt a prick of envy.

The only bulbs she'd ever grown indoors were paperwhites, which flowered easily in a sunny window. Hyacinths, she knew, required chilling: each bulb wedged into the narrow opening of a forcing jar so that the tips of its twine-like roots barely grazed the water, and the jars then placed somewhere cold and dark for several weeks before gradually being moved to ever brighter and warmer rooms. There was something proud, almost impudent, about the way these hyacinths stood there, so erect, in that perfectly clean clay pot with its matching drip tray, all dressed up in the green bow, and no one to look at them but Laura. The tops of the bulbs, just visible above the moist, loamy soil, reminded her of three small, clenched fists, while each tiny blue or purple blossom on its crowded spear was a flawless star.

That's when the smell hit her.

She'd forgotten the smell of hyacinths, their cloying, almost sour earthiness. An image rose in her mind of a young woman, tall and poised, coming out of a wet field, her arms filled with wildflowers and, swinging across her back, a long, thick braid. Laura shuddered, as if at a bad memory, though it wasn't a memory at all, more like a dredged-up association, or a feeling.

A homemade card was tucked behind the pot: just a square of speckled linen paper and a greeting in dark purple ink. Laura's reading glasses were in her purse, but that didn't matter. She knew the handwriting.

"Hey." Daniel had combed his wet bangs neatly to one side and was wearing a vintage rugby shirt she'd bought him on Saint-Laurent. The white collar was a little frayed, and the stripes, she couldn't help noticing, were the same purple as the ink.

She twirled the card, trying to sound lighthearted and amused. "So, when did your dad and Bryony get back together?"

"Don't know." How quickly he slipped back into the familiar gruff wariness. "He brought that over last night. I didn't ask him."

"You didn't ask him why he brought you a present from his old girlfriend?" Laura reached into her purse for her glasses case.

"Mom, don't."

Silently, she read: *Sweet Daniel, I've so missed our chats about books and life.* Drawn beneath this greeting was a swooping *B* and a skinny heart surrounded with tiny radiating lines—to suggest what? That Bryony's heart still beat for Daniel? That all these years she had been pining for him?

ONLY THREE ACTUALLY—YET AMONG THE HAPPI-est years Laura could remember anymore. After Bryony kicked Mike out, she'd felt younger, lighter, more care-free. More compassionate too, including toward her ex-husband whom she now exchanged texts with and on occasion fed. She'd felt as if she were falling in love again. Not with Mike, God forbid (though several of their old friends had floated this idea), but with herself. Or if not that exactly (Laura was skeptical of self-love), with the even keel of her life now. She would pause in the middle of some small ritual, buying her morning coffee near the teaching hospital where she worked as an administrator in student affairs, or filling the dishwasher after a dinner with her son and his dad, and feel this elation waft through her. Relief—yet also gratitude and oddly mostly to Bryony, who in the winter of Daniel's final year of high school, after all that she'd put Laura through, had done the unexpected and then as good as vanished.

Of course, she continued to dream about her. Laura could have filled a book with her Bryony dreams, although they were all variations on a theme and so transparent that she no longer bothered mentioning them to anyone. She would discover with a pang of anxious acquiescence, for instance, midway through a dream of something else entirely, that Daniel was getting married and to a young woman she'd never met. Only when she arrived at the barn in the countryside where the wedding was to take place, hoping to see Mike at least in the crowd of strangers, she'd find Bryony there ahead of her, looking like a bride herself in a long ivory silk slip with spaghetti straps that showed off her lightly freckled shoulders. And it would turn out that Bryony had done the catering, had even made the wedding cake, was best of friends already with the bride and both her parents. Or, worse, the girl he was marrying would turn out to be Bryony's younger daughter, Amber, and Laura would wake with sweat prickling down her back, thinking of her grandchildren who would now be also Bryony's.

That was the thing: if Bryony had been satisfied with Mike alone, Laura might have adjusted to her presence over time. But Bryony had not been satisfied. She'd set out to woo Laura's only child away from her as well (or so at least it had seemed, as she'd often felt compelled to qualify). That first Christmas, when he was ten, Bryony knitted him mittens, weaving in eight different-coloured stripes of yarn, and another year a sea-green Portuguese fisherman's sweater that Daniel wore constantly. Then there were the elaborate craft projects she sent him home with, the box of baby frogs Laura had to explain to him they couldn't keep, the books (Bryony's name carelessly penned inside), the mixed CDs with the personalized liner notes, the demo she helped him make in grade eleven. All the life advice that contradicted or subtly undermined Laura's own. Why not take a gap year? Go out West and plant trees or pick peaches, as her daughter Ivy had done? Or explore his songwriting? He could live with her and Mike in Hudson. They had so much space, and Daniel was so creative.

Mike in those years curiously receded, becoming for Bryony, it seemed, more of an adjunct or accessory. Sometimes at a crowded Christmas party, Laura would glimpse her ex standing mute beside his ever-animated new partner, in his ridiculous flowered shirt and bowler hat, and feel almost sorry for him. Her heart had clenched, however, each time Daniel drove off with his dad for a weekend at that house in Hudson, with its arty messiness and the dogs and the two adoring older stepsisters and Bryony, always Bryony, hovering over him, whispering to him, making him special meals, taking him for long walks. But what could she do? She often faltered describing Bryony's encroachments. They sounded so trivial put into words. Even her closest friends had asked whether she might be over-emotionalizing, impugning motive where there was none. Bryony surely was only trying to be a nice stepmom. Why shouldn't she knit him mittens? Why not lend him books?

WALKING PAST HER PARKED CAR, SHE STOLE A glance at her son, so handsome with his newly shaggy hair, the blue bomber jacket and mismatched cashmere scarf he'd wound around his neck rendering him even more adorable in her eyes. They'd made up in the hall, Daniel apologizing for his grumpiness and Laura for her sarcasm, but she knew they were both still worrying about the hyacinths.

The weather was also no longer so cheerful. Clouds had moved in, drawing attention to the drabness of the street, its narrow strips of yard with nothing poking up yet through the dirt. The garbage everywhere: pizza boxes, plastic bags leached of colour, the synthetic seaweed and neon pebbles from a discarded fish tank. A brown Christmas tree with a single piece of tinsel plastered to its stump. Laura thrust her hands into the sleeves of the light spring coat she'd grabbed on her way out the door in a flush of mistaken confidence.

"April is the cruellest month," she said.

Daniel grinned back at her. He'd read "The Waste Land" for the first time this semester for a modern poetry class, and although he didn't know it yet, a copy of Eliot's *Collected Poems* was inside the gift bag over Laura's arm.

"So where are we going?" she asked, struggling to match his stride.

The difference in their heights didn't normally bother her, but today it added to her sense of being off-kilter. She remembered watching Bryony cross her yard once to grab a dog's collar, her movements strong and fluid, rootless like a man's.

"I think you'll really like it," Daniel said. "It just opened and has all these plants."

"Oh, that sounds perfect."

They'd turned off the last of the Plateau side streets and were heading up Saint-Laurent. She searched her memory for when she'd last received a text from Mike. Two days ago: he'd wanted to know when she was taking Daniel out to lunch. Had Bryony known Laura would be stopping by Daniel's apartment? Were the hyacinths meant for her, to let her know that Bryony was back?

Once, when Laura was waiting for Daniel in her car at the bottom of that long driveway in Hudson, Bryony had suddenly opened the front passenger door and slid in beside her. Hi Laura, she'd said, sticking her face in close the way she always did at end-of-year assemblies and soccer games, insisting she be recognized. A wry smile trembling on her full lips as if she thought Laura's stunned glance, the way her hands flew up to the steering wheel was funny. You know, she'd continued before Laura could tell her to get out, We're in relationship, you and me, and the sooner you accept—

"Here we are," Daniel said. He'd stopped in front of a nondescript black door flush with the sidewalk. "This is it."

Belladonna was written in an old-fashioned business script across the glass, though the gold lettering was so faint Laura could have easily walked right past. Once they'd stepped inside the cage-like entrance and were waiting for the hostess, she could see that the restaurant was not only packed but also surprisingly deep with exposed brick walls and pipes running this way and that across the ceiling, suggesting a past life as a garage or small textile factory. All the tables were metal and the seating a mix of wooden benches and school chairs. As her eyes adjusted, she noticed the plants Daniel had mentioned: hanging basket upon hanging basket of pothos, their twisting vines of heart-shaped leaves forming a thick, ragged curtain across a picture window she also hadn't noticed from the street. It was the plants, she realized, that made the restaurant so dark.

"Did you make a reservation?" she whispered.

"Don't worry," Daniel said, though he seemed tense.

If no one came in the next few minutes, she might suggest they try somewhere else, maybe that nice Italian place three or four blocks away—would he be hurt? But someone did come: a young woman in a short denim jumper whose expression under her blunt black bangs was about as welcoming as the furnishings. Laura couldn't make out over the noise what she and Daniel said to each other in French, but the hostess did eventually lead them to what looked like a steel teacher's desk in a back corner.

"You sit in, Mom, so you can see everything," Daniel offered.

What she saw, once she'd wedged her coat behind her as a cushion, was a naked mannequin suspended between two ceiling pipes. Its smooth hairless head was tilted menacingly toward her, a dollar store lei drooping from its neck. Ugly plastic dolls hung as well from the ceiling, along with antique globes, disco balls, and lots of loose wires painted the same olive green as the pipes and left simply to dangle. On another day, Laura might have enjoyed this kitschy in-your-face décor, which reminded her of a Toronto bar she'd gone to a couple of times with Mike when they were first dating. But there was something almost aggressive about all those weird objects clustered up there together, and she remembered now how that bar from her twenties had unnerved her too, made her feel as if she'd stumbled into a room belonging to a crazy person and that if she stayed much longer, she might go crazy too.

"Very cool," she said to Daniel.

"Do you like it?"

"Yes, it's really funky," she said, though she knew he could sense the strain under her bright tone. "So, shall we order some wine?"

"I don't think they do wine. Just beer and cocktails. If you don't like it here, Mom, we can go somewhere else."

"No, no. I'm fine." She placed her glasses case on the table. "Is that the menu?"

Daniel slid between them a narrow piece of stained brown parchment. On one side under the heading Smør-rebrød were listed five different open-faced sandwiches. On the other about the same number of cocktails, with clever names like Lover's Heart and Marriage of Figaro but strangely unappetizing combinations of ingredients. She stared blankly at each description, unable to stop picturing Bryony in the studio of the century farmhouse that she'd shared briefly with her daughters' father, Jeremy, and then for another nine years with Mike. Surrounded by her drying presses, her moulds and deckles, the plastic bins filled with Japanese fibres, locally gathered ferns and grasses; humming as she tied the green ribbon in a bow and chose an ink for her fountain pen that complemented the hyacinths.

A waiter stood over them. He was small and compactly muscular with a shaved head and the same laconic air as the hostess. Laura tried to get him to recommend a cocktail, but he kept repeating with an insistence bordering on condescension that it depended on what she liked. In the end, she ordered a Marriage of Figaro and Daniel ordered a craft beer. When the drinks arrived, they exchanged sips. Daniel's, a maple stout, heavy and sweet, while hers so tart she had to be careful not to make a face. At the bottom of the glass, there was an actual half fig skewered on a tiny plastic sword.

When the waiter returned for their food order, he asked what she thought of the cocktail and Laura gushed that it was wonderful.

"Do the sandwiches come with salad?" she asked hopefully.

But they didn't.

"I think there's a garnish that's sort of salad-y," Daniel said.

Laura took another sip of her Marriage of Figaro, then placed the gift bag on the table. "So," she said desperate to salvage some of her earlier happiness. "Are you going to open your present?"

"I thought new running shoes were my present."

"This is just a little extra something." As he pulled out her battered Faber edition, she added, "It's my copy from university. It has all my old notes. You'll probably find them pretty silly."

The cover with its grey-toned portrait of the poet in profile had all these white marks as if someone had scratched his pensive brow with a fingernail. Inside several of the pages had come loose.

Daniel read from where the book fell open. *"What are the roots that clutch, what branches grow Out of this stony rubbish?"*

"I loved 'The Waste Land,' but I don't think I understood it at all," Laura said. "What did I say on that page?"

"Well, you circled *roots*. But I can't read your handwriting, Mom. It's too small."

Suddenly, she remembered. "There are hyacinths in 'The Waste Land,' aren't there?"

Daniel turned to the next page and read solemnly: *"You gave me Hyacinths first a year ago; They called me the hyacinth girl. —Yet when we came back, late, from the hyacinth garden, your arms full and your hair wet—"*

"Can I see?" Laura took the book and read the stanza to herself, including the quotation in German that her note from thirty years ago said was from *Tristan und Isolde*. The old malaise swept through her. The sense that there would always be those who got to live in beauty, coming back late with their arms full, and those that didn't. "Did you know your father was back with Bryony?"

"Mom, do we have to?"

"I just think it's weird that he didn't breathe a word to me."

He rolled his eyes. "Well, that shouldn't really surprise you."

This was one of the solaces of the past three years: she and Daniel had begun to talk about those earlier ones. He'd been such a quiet child and withdrawn teenager, and she too had held back, not wanting to prejudice him against his father, but also afraid, so afraid, that by saying something angry or bitter that got repeated she might send him running to Bryony. A year or so ago, though, after he switched majors to English, they'd begun opening up about the affair, parsing their memories and responses from that time as they might a novel or a poem, often over a bottle of wine.

Laura had shared how the first time she saw the two of them together, at that reception after a choral society

Christmas concert, she'd known. How it was like look-ing at one of those drawings in a children's activity book where you're supposed to spot what's wrong, except she couldn't put her finger on it, not yet. Just that Mike seemed oddly nervous as Laura crossed the room to be introduced, and the tall woman in the short black cock-tail dress by his side not at all. A gifted mezzo-soprano, he'd said. Also an artist, a papermaker. Recently moved to Hudson with her husband, an art historian. Two lovely teenaged daughters. And Bryony, whose thick auburn hair was pinned up that night in a loose bun, tendrils of which curled artfully against her cheeks, had clinked her wineglass against his and said in that grav-elly voice that would tunnel its way into Laura's dreams, And this must be the wife.

They'd also talked about Daniel's relationship with his stepmom. He'd acknowledged how in the beginning he enjoyed all the attention lavished upon him but how later he began to feel uncomfortable, especially when Bryony would show up unexpectedly at the cafe where he worked and hang around for hours, chatting to his coworkers, reaching out to touch his arm as he walked past. Even in middle school, when Bryony had had the most influence over him, he'd sensed she might be try-ing to subtly hurt his mother, or at least that she didn't care if Laura was hurt, but he hadn't known what he should do. How could you? Laura had said. You were so young, and you needed your dad.

Today, though, she sensed a returning reticence. Dread even, as if he wanted to protect them from her.

"So, how long would you say?" she asked, the liquor making her reckless. "A week? A month? A year?" And when he looked away, "Did Bryony know you'd just read T. S. Eliot? Is that why she brought you hyacinths?"

"Don't be crazy, Mom," Daniel said.

The waiter was approaching. As he set down the plates with the open-faced sandwiches and flourished a pepper shaker, she said nothing. Then she couldn't help herself. "That's what your father used to say."

"I'm sorry," he said. "It's just—"

She picked up her fork and knife and sliced through her cold asparagus spear into the square of black rye. Trying not to sound petty and manipulative. "It's okay. It has nothing to do with me. I see that."

Daniel sighed and picked up his own cutlery. The birthday lunch was ruined. Bryony's hyacinths had ruined it, but also Laura herself. She knew that was what he was thinking, that she was jealous—when what she felt was a dry, stony, hopeless rage.

"Do you know where the women's washroom is?" she asked.

"By the bar, I think."

Squeezing out from behind their table, she tried not to notice how his hand reached for his phone.

THAT FIRST TIME, THEY KEPT HER IN THE DARK for eight months. Images from those evenings she spent in Hudson, asking Bryony polite questions about her latest project, the course she was teaching in the fibre arts program at Concordia on the properties of pulp, the heirloom tomatoes she grew from seed and canned, still had the power to undo her. How gauche she'd felt in the presence of this older musical friend of her husband's who seemed so gifted at so many things and who never asked her any questions in return. How dull and sexless. In these images, she is almost always seated, planted on the same sagging armchair in Bryony's living room, with its faux fur rugs and rattan coffee table, its mustard walls covered in inked drawings, unable to move or even look away from what she recognized at the margins of her consciousness as desire spreading stealthily like tubers under a placid lawn. Again, nothing she could point to with any certainty. An arch glance; a longer, seemingly more tender one. Mike leaping to his feet to help Bryony fetch more firewood from the pile outdoors. A glimpse of the two of them bounding across the yard, arms nearly touching. And once when Bryony insisted that he and Laura stay the night so they could open more wine, an odd moment at the top of the stairs when it appeared as if a subtle realignment had already taken place and she was meant to go with Jeremy, whose passions appeared so mild, so burdened with caution. Like her own.

Paper leads a double life, Bryony explained one night when Laura, to cover over some gap in conversation, asked what drew her to it. There's the boring surface life, she said. The one we know already, that's functional and conventional. And then there's the deeper hidden inner life that's connected to nature and antiquity and to beauty, which the artist feels an almost sacred duty to explore.

And this, Laura realized in the semi-darkness of her cubicle in Belladonna's, was what enraged her. Not the duplicity, the garden-variety adultery and betrayal of marriage vows, not the loss of a husband she no longer even thought about in that way, but the degree to which she'd acquiesced to this idea of a superior hidden life. Let it unfurl inside her, leaf after greedy leaf, even as she saw through Bryony's pretensions, saw how she used beauty and art to cloak her own shallow self-absorption. Yet still unable to counter this sense of *being* less, of being judged and judging herself as *less*. A hole plunging open at her feet and dragging her down, holding her firmly in place where she did not want to be—so that all she was left with were the flimsy darts of the injured wife.

Standing at the washroom sink, she dared herself to look up, only for the mirror in its kitschy oval gilt frame to fling back the same old laughing retort. We're in relationship, Bryony told her in the car that day, the dropped article lending the words, even then, a crazed clairvoyance. And the sooner you accept this the better, for Daniel.

When Laura got back to the table, he was texting.

"Who's that?" she asked, and immediately wished she hadn't. "I'm sorry."

Daniel slid the phone back into his jacket pocket. "I'm sorry too, Mom."

He leaned forward, laced his fingers together, glanced at his beer glass. "There's something I need to tell you.

I should have before. I'm really, really sorry. I know you don't like her—"

"It's okay." She patted his wrist through the rugby shirt, steeled herself.

"I don't know all the details," he said. "She's—" He was struggling, trapped again between the two of them. "She's waiting for more results. But the thing is it might be too late, it might have already spread. I'm sorry I didn't say anything when you saw the flowers. Dad didn't want me to, or maybe it was her, I don't know. I'm not even sure they're back together. She may have just reached out to him because—"

LATER, SHE WOULD REMEMBER THE WATERY RINGS their glasses made on the metal tabletop and a woozy feeling when they stood to leave, a consciousness of her rumpled spring coat as she passed under all those wire tendrils into sudden, unexpected sunlight, so bright that for a moment her eyes failed her—yet little else of what either of them said in Belladonna's.

Retracing their steps along the same side streets to where Laura's car was parked, they talked earnestly about Daniel's courses, his exam schedule, a gig he had coming up at a coffeehouse on campus. Then they were standing beside the car, and he was hugging her good-bye, and she was watching him walk away from her with the book of poems in his hand.

She opened the driver's door, placed her purse on the passenger seat, and fitted the key into the ignition, then sat for a moment looking over the steering wheel at a small bare maple sapling on the verge. She knew she should be feeling something: empathy surely for this woman who must be so afraid. Or, if those gentler feelings had been truly rooted out of her, for her daughters. Some grim satisfaction at least, a crueller version of the relief she'd woken to three years ago. Suspicion even, for was it not possible that Bryony was exaggerating the seriousness of her illness?

Instead, she found herself thinking about the striped mittens Daniel brought home from Hudson that first Christmas when he was ten. How she'd dreaded having to see or touch them, but also how she could never bring herself to suggest he wear his warmer store-bought fleece ones, not as long as he preferred his Bryony mittens. How she used to even arrange them on the floor for him, with his snow jacket and boots and toque, as if she wanted him to wear them. And in a way maybe she had. Although he was always leaving them places, she remembered now. She would think one was lost for good, only to find it frozen on the driveway or squirrelled under the passenger seat with the empty juice boxes and torn granola-bar wrappers, the loosely balled Kleenexes. Or the mother of one of his friends would call: We've got Daniel's mittens here. They're so beautiful. Did you knit them? No, she would have to say. Not me. And how then one day they were just gone.

Maeve

I MET MAEVE AT CLATTER CHATTER. NOT THAT anyone called it that except the two older moms in dryer-worn turtlenecks who organized it. The fifties-greeting-card gaiety probably reminded the rest of us too much of what we'd given up, for there was little chatter in that basement room that wasn't mired in the excreting and teething and sleeping regimens of under-fives. As for the clatter, it was deafening. Crayons striking the bottom of a cookie tin like rounds of artillery. A continual pop-pop of push-dogs and push-ducks. Rattling cranks and levers on beat-up activity boards: little blue hare smashing into little green turtle again, again. The ungodly screech of the Fisher-Price phone as its bulbous eyes rolled back.

Still, the hours I spent there, downing cup after cup of acrid filter coffee, cutting out paper shapes of rainbows and fishes and daisy petals with gluey scissors were, in truth, the highlight of my week. Thursday-morning playgroup was Joshua's and my one engagement: a clear circle of breath in all the steamy formlessness. Pushing his stroller past the deserted double driveways of my neighbours, my step as brisk as when I too had had a job to drive to, I would sing to him. *The itsy-bitsy spider crawled up the waterspout. Down came the rain and washed the spider out.* After all, I *could* have gone back to my job full-time. I could have put my baby in daycare as Chris and I had initially planned. Yet if that baby woke on a Thursday with a runny nose, if his forehead still felt warm after his Gerber mixed cereal and he flung his sippy cup on the floor, if he cried instead of playing with his trains so that Mommy couldn't drink her coffee, down came the panic again, and I would seize him from his high chair or the floor and hold him tight, sometimes a little too tight.

Maeve at this time—the only time I knew her, nearly thirty years ago—would have experienced no such doubts. While most of us shrank from the Mommy Wars—reassuring colleagues we'd be back, taking on contracts to keep a hand in—she flaunted her choice to stay at home like a warrior queen. She was still proudly breast-feeding both her daughters and, when not carrying about the younger one in a homemade sling, purple with gold stars, ruled our little playgroup from its tank-like nursing chair, issuing edicts on breast vs. bottle, natural vs. epidural, cloth vs. paper. Bethany, who like Joshua was nearly three, would sometimes get up from the blocks corner and stand beside this chair, and Maeve would pull her breast from Lydia's snail mouth and draw her first-born close.

Other moms draped baby blankets over their shoulders and called it nursing, but Maeve's blouses were always undone, the flaps of her bra yanked down so that we could all see the raised brown tips of her nipples. In Africa, she said, where there's no taboo against attachment parenting, women breastfeed their children until six or seven. She herself did it in the mall food court. Once a security guard suggested she try the family room and she told him to fuck off.

"He actually put his hand on my chest," she told me. "The pervert."

This was in my kitchen. Lydia slumped placidly at her feet while we waited for the coffee machine to finish dripping, the two older ones secreted away upstairs as usual. I never would have gravitated to her on my own. Maeve reminded me too much of student-activist types I'd observed in the early eighties: handing out leaflets in the college cafeteria, cutting class for marches. Always so sure of being on the righteous side. She liked to goad her fellow playgroup moms, claim that bottle-feeding makes kids obese or call daycares concentration camps, then stare boldly over the fluffy heads of our toddlers at the craft table. Not that any of us ever rose to the bait. We treated Maeve with the same meek unquestioning acceptance as we did the lone dad stinking of weed who let his twins dump all the puzzle pieces on the carpet or the sullen teenager whose stretched tank tops suggested another was already on the way. Yet

I *never* would have let her into my home if Joshua had not been so infatuated.

"Our children seem to be inseparable," Maeve observed one day as we filled the Duplo bin together during tidy-up.

I'd already noticed Bethany whisper to Joshua and knew that soon would come the agonizing pretense of not seeing him, the standing about with his snowsuit and boots asking him to please come out wherever you are, my bright tone wearing down on their combined resistance. I was glad my usually shy son had found a friend but wished it could have been one of the boys, so gentle and uncomplicated, driving Dinky cars along the empty toy shelves. Not Bethany with her flaming cheeks and small, defiant mouth pressed up against his ear.

When Joshua and Bethany refused to come out of the baby pit, Maeve shrugged. "Where do you live? We haven't got anything on."

They never did. On those rare occasions when Joshua and I were busy after playgroup, Maeve would simply carry on to the mall, buy the girls Happy Meals, then rifle through sidewalk-sales racks until it was time to drive home and start supper for her husband. When it was her turn for snack, she always brought homemade zucchini muffins or a sliced cranberry loaf, still warm, in a basket lined with a clean checked cloth. She baked her own bread, grew tomatoes from seed, sewed most of the girls' and her own clothes, so the fast-food lunches came as a surprise. The first chink in her Earth Mama armour. And there were other chinks. She regularly praised her own thrift, for instance, yet ordered Bethany's brightly patterned leotards from an expensive US catalogue and splurged each week on a new romance novel from Coles, concealing the fat paperback in a silk book cover she'd sewn specifically for this purpose.

"Carl is the classic absent-minded professor, he never notices a thing." She laughed, her cheeks a flush of pinpricks.

What Maeve got out of our afternoons together I never gave much thought to then. I was too grateful for her solid back against my kitchen counter, her strident voice filling up the hours between noon and four. I knew I was supposed to play with Joshua—push Thomas and Percy back and forth on the floor, make up stories for his stuffed animals—but felt at ease only when there was laundry to gather up, toddler undershirts to fold, or Maeve to listen to. She regarded me mostly, I suppose, as a little sister she could tutor in the arts of mothering, though Bethany and Joshua were just a month apart and Maeve six years my junior. Maybe it was that I had only the one or that I still worked part-time. At any rate, she lent me books on attachment parenting and easy sewing projects, catalogues of wooden toys, a food mill to make baby food (For your next one). And in return, I let her grandstand in my kitchen.

"Don't Ferberize him," she urged when I admitted we were leaving Joshua in his crib to cry it out. "Ferber," she scoffed, "is manna from heaven for career moms, lets them get their beauty rest guilt-free. Co-sleeping is the norm in most of the world. It's only in North America that we lock up babies in separate rooms."

The girls slept with her and Carl in what she called their family bed. "It's so much healthier," she counselled. "You and Chris should try it."

"You don't find it affects your sex life?" I asked.

But Maeve was impervious to irony.

Another time she told me that the mainstream child-care experts were waging a full-out war against children. It was all about raising little cookie-cutter boys and girls who would play along with corporate America. This was why the media gave airtime to Nazis like Ferber.

"Where do you think they get their funding?" she said, and when I didn't answer, "Big surprise. Pampers."

Only once, when she noticed an official-looking document on the counter, did she ask about my freelance work, and I belittled it, saying, "It's just a contract."

"I have a master's in urban planning," she volunteered, tracing a finger across the cover page. "But then I got pregnant, and Carl and I agreed that it's better for a mother to be home."

I WAS IN THAT HOME ONLY ONCE. MAEVE HAD asked often enough, starting that first afternoon in my kitchen, but I'd always found a reason to defer: Joshua's nap, a pressing deadline, the long drive. Maybe I sensed that we were safer where we were, our difference neutralized by the steady gurgling of my coffee machine. Yet

I must have recognized that my noncompliance also carried risks. At any rate, one afternoon in early April, I brought Joshua for a playdate.

They lived out past the airport, in a stretch of dilapidated farmhouses and modest bungalows with sun-bleached ride-on toys strewn across muddy lawns and every so often a satellite dish tipped to one side like a dropped bowl. The drive took almost an hour, and I wondered how Maeve could bear it. There wasn't even a gas station convenience store nearby. But living in the country had been a fantasy of Carl's. He wouldn't even let her look at other listings, she'd said. I knew the house was over a century old and very large (Maeve had joked that it was like living in Jamaica Inn). Still, I wasn't prepared for the four chimneys or the crumbling two-storey barn that clung precariously from one end. When we pulled up behind her silver van, Maeve was just emerging from this barn with Lydia hoisted on her hip and Bethany holding out a large wicker basket. They were all wearing long prairie-style dresses under their snow jackets along with rubber boots, and their cheeks were lashed with cold.

As I unbelted Joshua, Maeve called out with a trill of pride, "We've been collecting eggs." And Bethany tipped her basket forward so I could see.

Inside, the two older children kicked off their boots into a loose checkerboard of running shoes, tiny sandals, and men's loafers, and fled upstairs. Maeve led me through a cavernous dining room so crowded with heavy, dark furniture it reminded me of one of those highway antique emporiums that so often disappoint. Pressed against one wall was a huge fish tank that gave out a low roar. Lydia reached a hand toward the glass.

Maeve paused long enough for me to glimpse a flit or two of tail and fin, a tiny gold stare from out of the dark. She groaned. "Carl's."

"They're beautiful," I said.

She snorted and pointed to a brown lump hovering near the bottom. "What about that one? Do you think it's beautiful?"

The fish, she reiterated when we were sitting at her kitchen table with our coffee cups and a plate of fresh-baked muffins, were Carl's alone. He'd insisted on buying the tank when they first moved in. She hated that he'd put it in the dining room, hated its racket, hated that she was the one who had to clean it. The Chinese algae eater was supposed to help with that by sucking up the slime, but she was pretty sure Carl bought it just to piss her off. She hated watching the hideous creature feed, the way its mouth got stuck on rocks or against the glass front. Once it escaped out the top of the aquarium, and she had to pick it up off the floor with her bare hands. And Carl had had the nerve to criticize her for not being more careful.

To the extent that I thought about him at all, I'd pictured Maeve's Carl as one of those tall, gangly academic types whose hair is already receding by thirty: earnest but ineffectual. He was a biologist, into earthworms apparently. The fish tank, I decided, must have been one of those small acts of marital resistance, like Maeve's clandestine paperbacks.

MAEVE

"How did the two of you meet?" I asked.

She had Lydia on her lap and was sculpting something for her from a still-warm batch of play dough. I could see the pot she'd made it in next to the sink as well as a stack of cereal bowls stained orange from Kraft Dinner, a blackened muffin tin. Most of the cupboard doors were thrown open, revealing a jumble of cans and boxes, which surprised me even more than the Happy Meals. Somehow, I had expected Maeve, with her firm views on staying at home, to keep a tidy house.

"At a pub," she answered. "I came in wearing this sexy black dress from Le Château, all lace and really tight. These super high leather boots." I was amused by how quickly I could picture sturdy Maeve as this black-lace eighties dominatrix. "I already knew that I wanted him," she continued, placing a perfectly formed pink swan in front of Lydia and unable to resist a smile at her own artistry. "I'd seen him around campus and knew he went to the grad pub on Friday nights. He used to shoot pool with this gang of pre-meds. That was before he went the academic route." She rolled her eyes, Carl's assistant-professor salary a sore point. "Anyway, I bought the outfit specially and got my roommate to come with me. Only she ended up having to crash at a friend's place because Carl, he couldn't wait to rip that dress off me. What about you and Chris?"

"Oh, nothing so exciting." I never shared like Maeve. I prided myself, in fact, on how little she really knew about me. "Friends through work. That's an amazing swan, by the way."

Maeve wanted to show me the rest of the house, so once we'd finished our coffees, she lifted Lydia onto her hip again and led me back past the fish tank to the stairs, which were littered with Zellers flyers and tiny plastic barrettes in the shapes of daisies and butterflies.

On the second-floor landing, she waved at the long hallway of shut doors. "Bethany loves to play hotel up here. She gets all decked out in her dress-up clothes and has me serve her lunch in a different room each day."

"I guess all that extra space is handy for visitors," I said.

"Oh, I plan to have more children," she said, a glint of challenge in her voice. I'd mentioned once in my kitchen that Chris and I weren't so sure we'd have another one. Why not? she'd demanded, and I changed the subject, asked how she got her muffins to rise so beautifully.

She took me into the girls' rooms first. Bethany's contained only a toddler mattress half buried under blankets and rumpled dresses and a low pressboard shelving unit spewing picture books onto the dusty softwood floor. Also scattered about this floor were drawings—most of these just a wobbly circle or one or two thick lines—as well as coloured pencils and markers and a great quantity of broken crayons. Lydia's baby room too seemed merely a dumping ground for clothes and books and her sister's scribblings. Next to the change table, an over-stuffed diaper pail gave off the smell of days-old urine mixed with plastic.

"Nice big rooms," I said.

She shrugged, and again I sensed the challenge in her voice. "The girls sleep with us. Their rooms are just for playing in. I don't bother much with maintenance. I'd rather read to them or do a craft."

Next, she showed me the master bedroom, which was dominated by their family bed: a massive mahogany four-poster, Beanie Babies and Barbies staring blankly from its twisted sheets. A drift of greyish fabric by the window appeared to be one of Maeve's nursing bras, the cups turned inside out. Below, I could glimpse her frozen garden, a few misshapen tomato cages from last year's harvest still left standing.

"Do you think the kids are okay?" I asked.

"Obviously," she snapped, hitching Lydia higher up her hip. "Bethany and Lydia play all the time on their own."

She closed this door more quickly than she had the ones to the girls' rooms, then pointed at the door to her sewing room across the hall but didn't invite me in. My awareness of Joshua's absence was beginning to throb like a phantom limb. I'd never minded him running off with Bethany at my house, but here there seemed more dangers. Like Maeve's sewing machine. Did she think to lock that room? Or the barn. Was there a way of getting to it from the second floor? But I knew better than to ask.

WE FOUND THEM IN CARL'S HOME OFFICE, THE giggling audible even before Maeve turned the knob. They were hiding underneath his desk, which was huge and dark and ugly like all the furniture. Against one wall, I noticed a metal shelving unit stuffed with faded brown file folders and what looked like stacks of science journals. Across from this was a couch with a cushion loosely stuffed inside a pillowcase and on a small round table a cloudy glass.

"Bethany, come out, right now," Maeve said. "Joshua's mommy has been very worried."

"No!"

Maeve set Lydia down on the floor, then folded her arms. "You know Papa doesn't like you in here."

"Papa doesn't care. It's you he doesn't like in here."

"That's enough backtalk, young lady. Do you want a timeout?"

"NO!"

"I'm starting to count. Ten." She tapped her foot. "Nine. Do you hear me, Bethany? Eight."

But Bethany had begun to sing. "I looove you. You looove—"

"Seven."

Now Joshua was piping in. "We're a haaappy—"

"Six. Five. Four."

They were singing faster. "I-love-you-you-love-me—" Then louder, drowning out Maeve's *three*. "WE'RE A HAPPY—"

I knew there would be no time-out, that Bethany would win this battle as I'd guessed by now that she did most. For Maeve's sake, though, I called out feebly, "Joshua, listen to Bethany's mommy."

"LY—"

"Two," Maeve said. "Okay, one and three-quarters. One and a half."

MAEVE

Bars of late-afternoon shadow were advancing across the softwood. It could have been four o'clock or six. Suddenly, I felt so incredibly tired. All I wanted was to lie down on Carl's office floor, to press my cheek against its dark, dusty coolness. Instead, I swayed on my heels, waiting for Maeve to give in.

Yet, when it came, her retreat was so complete I felt embarrassed for us both. "I've got cookies!" she announced. "M&M chip."

"Can we have four each?"

"Yes, and you can have your apple juice in Mama's special teapot."

Satisfied with these spoils, Bethany elbowed her way out from beneath the desk. For a moment, I thought she was naked, and my legs went soft. When she scrambled to her feet, I saw that she still had on her panties at least and that the jagged square of red cloth tied around her neck was meant to be a cape. With her bright cheeks and tumble of soft brown curls, she looked like a cherubic Wonder Woman. All that was missing her golden rope.

But I was now more focused on Joshua crawling out behind her. At home, our dress-up clothes consisted of a firefighter's hat, a wand, and a couple of plastic swords, so it's possible that I might have pressed my lips together, even wondered fleetingly what Chris would think. That's when Maeve laughed: whether at Joshua or at me, I couldn't tell at first. The laugh was not a nice one. The realization crept over me that this was a test, a test of my mothering, and that Maeve was watching to see how I would react. Bethany too appeared flushed with anticipation, and even Lydia made gleeful little squeaks as my son twirled in his tutu, a matching tiara tucked behind his ears.

"Joshua, it's time to go home," I said, avoiding Maeve's eyes as I reached for his sweatpants. "Where's your shirt, sweetie?" I tugged the white tulle skirt down about his legs and removed the hairpiece and, when he started to whine, repeated, "It's time. Daddy will be missing us."

At the landing, Maeve said, "You know, it's perfectly normal to gender role-play."

She smiled again, and I saw the same animal delight light up her face as when she'd placed the swan in front of Lydia, when Bethany tipped the basket full of eggs. Maeve, I saw more clearly, was not my friend. We weren't even comrades in the same struggle. All along, she'd only been waiting to triumph over me.

To find my chink.

I squeezed Joshua's hand so hard he started to whimper. When he slipped on a stair, I squeezed harder. When he slipped again, I dragged him down the next two. But before we could reach the bottom, the front door opened, and a man stood in my way.

Bethany bolted past us and threw her arms around his thighs. "Papa!" Carl was short. That was all I could take in at first. Shorter than Maeve by a good three inches, and anything but gangly. "Mama said I had to have a time-out and I said no!"

"Oh, you did, did you?" His voice seemed oddly flat.

"Yes, and now we're going to have cookies and apple-juice tea."

"Cookies just before dinner? That doesn't sound like a very good plan. What's Mama thinking of?"

He took off a brown fake-leather bomber jacket and bent to remove galoshes: the kind with zippers, though Carl's had been left to flap open. I couldn't stop staring at his stomach, which as he stood up again rose blimp-like between a pair of old-fashioned suspenders. His checked dress shirt was missing a button, exposing a tuft of coarse black hair. His throat, however, was milky white, his mouth wide and sensuous.

Carl appeared to be taking me in as well, his lip curling in a way that seemed to strip me of my two post-secondary degrees and decade in the workforce.

"Hello, Maeve's friend," he said.

Then he fixed his eyes higher up the stairs. "Supper all ready, I suppose?"

This irony Maeve appeared to get just fine. All she said, though, was, "You're early."

It might have been the drop in her voice, or something in his torpid stance at the bottom of the stairs, or just the deepening shadows that reminded me for an instant, as I grabbed Joshua's boots and carried him outside, of that other, older war.

NOT LONG AFTERWARD, I TOOK A FULL-TIME position with an educational software company. Not as stimulating as the government job I'd given up, but

Chris and I agreed that we could use the second salary. We found Joshua a place in a highly recommended daycare near my office. The preschool class raised butterflies from chrysalides and released them in a special ceremony on the playground that parents were invited to. There was a reading corner and a puppet stage, though no dress-up clothes for fear of lice.

I wondered if Joshua would miss Bethany, but he was focused now on having playdates with William and Lucas, whose mothers were too busy for more than a few pleasantries at the door and never expected coffee. Yet one morning, about six months after I'd gone back to work, Maeve called. It was a provincial holiday—Remembrance Day, I believe—and she must have guessed that Joshua and I would both be home. She and the girls were heading into town, she said. Could they drop by? Bethany was always asking about Joshua. She didn't understand why he wasn't coming to playgroup anymore. I could hardly say no.

Lydia was the most changed. She was walking now, and her hair had grown in, in tiny white-blond ringlets. She'll be prettier than Bethany, I thought, looking at the two heads nestled against Maeve's wide hips. I'd wondered what Joshua and Bethany would make of one another, but after some unexpected shyness on her part and diffidence on his, and with some gentle prodding on mine (Why don't you show Bethany your new LEGO set?), they fled upstairs. I poured Maeve a cup of coffee and offered up a plate of the banana bread I'd bought the day before at the bakery in my building. Lydia wanted to draw, so I fetched some paper and a bucket of crayons from the family room.

When I got back to the kitchen, Maeve was removing a large plastic pencil box from her diaper bag. Inside must have been a hundred coloured pencils, each chiselled to a delicate point. Lying row upon row, they resembled a stockade, not the usual rough-barked kind but smooth, slender, brightly coloured. The pencils were almost too perfect, too beautiful to use. Lydia, however, immediately broke the light orange, pressing too hard on her paper. I felt like reaching out and rescuing the tiny tip before it rolled away, then closing the pencil box before she could grab another fistful.

Instead, I said, "Those are incredibly sharp coloured pencils."

Maeve smiled in the old way. "I sharpened them all yesterday. I sharpened every pencil in the house. It took me the whole morning."

Everything I disliked about the woman came flooding back. All the time I'd been at home, I'd felt so beholden, to my baby, to my husband, to some idea I had of how my house should look if I was going to be in it all day. I couldn't imagine spending a whole morning sharpening pencils while all around me chaos reigned, as it did at Maeve's.

"Really?" I said.

She shrugged. "I was depressed."

"Depressed? Whatever for?"

"I got pregnant. In the summer. It was an accident. Well, not entirely. The girls were at my parents'."

"Oh. Congratulations," I said. A little stiffly since Chris and I had recently decided not to try for another after all. Then noticing her wince, I recalibrated. "Oh, did you have a—? I'm so sorry."

"No, it's not that."

When I looked confused, she said, "I had an abortion." She bent her head then over Lydia's drawing. "What's this a pretty picture of?"

"Fish," said Lydia. "Rainbow fish. Like Papa's."

"Oh, how boo-ti-ful."

Maeve picked up a pencil and started filling in the wobbly shape with specks of turquoise. I picked up one too: salmon pink. I had friends, of course, who'd had abortions, but in their teens or early twenties when they were still essentially single or in school. The married women I knew, late starters like myself with middle-class careers, were more concerned about conceiving in the first place.

"You didn't want it then?" I said, thinking of all those extra rooms.

"Carl—" She glanced down again at Lydia's fish.

"He didn't?"

She put aside the turquoise pencil, picked up a lime-green one, then shook her head.

I knew she wanted me to ask more questions, that the air was charged with them and that these questions could be a call to arms, an appeal to some long-ago ideal of sisterhood with its sewing circles and home births, its consciousness-raising meetings in smoke-filled living rooms. But I kept my head down, kept colouring, and the moment passed.

MAEVE

When Lydia got down to play on the floor with the pencils, I brought over the coffee carafe and refilled our cups. We talked idly about the children, my new job, the other playgroup moms until it was noon by my kitchen clock. Guessing Maeve would want to stay for lunch, I made up an excuse, said Joshua had another playdate for the afternoon. Then I walked to the stairs and called him and Bethany down.

What went on in that marriage was not my problem. That's what I told myself as I watched Maeve squat in her big gathered skirt to put on Lydia's shoes and as she explained to Bethany that they had to go now, that Joshua had another friend coming. What could I have done anyway? I had enough on my plate, working full-time, looking after a three-and-a-half-year-old. I barely knew them. No, Maeve would be fine. She'd have to get over this disappointment, as she would others. As we all would have to. That's what I stuck to as I stood in my doorway and watched her nudge the two little girls in their flowered leotards down the walkway to her van. Lift Lydia into her booster seat and fasten her and Bethany's belts. Haul the heavy door across. Yet even as I waved good-bye, I could feel the smile rising to my lips. Not a nice smile. A smile not so different, in truth, from the one she'd turned on me at the top of her stairs. So maybe she'd taught me something after all.

Oh, she'd be fine all right, I told myself. Weren't all her pencils sharpened?

Wise Men Say

EVEN BEFORE HE SHOUTED HIS NAME, SHE'D known it wouldn't go anywhere. Penny wasn't a snob. Still, she couldn't help giving Nance a look when he approached them in the bar, so clearly the Halifax hoser in his squeaky-white Adidas knockoffs and Boston Bruins T-shirt, a tiny gold cross dangling at his throat.

I'm Al, he said—and when she went, Whaaat?—Al, AL FOLEY. She shot Nance another look. Al *what?* But he was kind of cute. Six feet or more, with big arms, loose brown hair, and surprisingly long eyelashes. And Penny was pretty wasted.

He told her he was twenty-two, that he lived with his parents on Pepperell Street and was starting electrician training in September. He also told her she was beautiful three times in Brandy's and, after they'd necked for awhile, piggybacked her home through the graveyard as she swung her sandals from one hand and kissed the back of his neck. They might have even done it in the field behind the junior high if he hadn't thought to ask if she was a virgin.

But the next day at the door, she noticed only the fleshiness of his lips as he leaned in to kiss her, much too wetly, on the mouth. She had no memory of saying he could come over yet no good reason not to let him inside. All she'd done since getting back for the summer, besides getting loaded with Nancy and her other high school friends, was laze about her father's house listening to her New Wave records. Just before he rang the bell, she'd been playing side A of *My Aim Is True*, the lights on the stereo making tiny star holes in the three-o'clock gloom. Elvis Costello, she said when he asked. Elvis who? You know, "Alison." She picked up the album cover from the couch. Al grinned. That's not Elvis.

The rest of the afternoon, she sat on his lap, recoiling at the coldness of his tongue but necking with him anyway, because she felt too hungover to think of a way out of it. By the time her father came home, he'd managed to remove her U of T sweatshirt and his own T-shirt and was slowly working his tongue, no longer so cold, toward the snap of her jeans. At the sound of the back door opening, they both sat up and began gingerly putting their tops back on. It was all so high school. She heard her father open a cupboard in the kitchen, bang the ice cube tray against the sink. I'm in the living room, she called out, and then, I thought I'd make hamburgers tonight. When he entered with his first Scotch of the night, she said, This is Al, and Al stood up from the couch and shook his hand. So what do you do, Al? her father asked. Presently unemployed, sir, he replied, shoving his fingers through his lank brown hair and rocking slightly on the Adidas knockoffs.

To Penny's annoyance, her father not only assumed Al was staying to dinner but also seemed to take a perverse liking to him. Molding semi-frozen beef into patties over the kitchen sink, she watched them through the window nursing their drinks on the patio. Al's stonewashed legs splayed open in the plaid lawn chair, her father still in his suit flicking ash on the bricks. What could they possibly find to talk about? But it appeared they were just as happy *not* talking. Al offered to take care of the barbecuing and helped Penny load the dishwasher, and afterward the three of them watched *The Love Boat* and *Fantasy Island* on channel 7. Whenever you want me to go, just tell me, Al said when her father finally shuffled off to bed, which made her want to scream because she'd wanted him to go all day. Still, something about the way he kissed her at the door (she was sitting on the wooden radiator box and he leaned in so gently) stirred her.

Al barely seemed to notice Penny's ambivalence. How on the phone she was always so noncommittal: Oh well, if you want to. How her lips were invariably dry when he kissed her. Yet this steadiness of purpose, so different from the waffling attentions of other guys, elicited in her a strange passivity. She went along with the flow, the way she supposed her mother must have once, before coming to her senses when Penny was eight and fleeing out West with an oil-and-gas man. She did like talking to Al, if only because it gave her a chance to try out her ideas on art, the meaning of life, whether love was even possible in an ironic age. She also liked the sex.

They had progressed from the living room to her bedroom, and he now removed all her clothes and did things to or for her (she was never quite sure which) that made her feel like a river flowing out to sea. At the last moment, though, he always rolled away. A year of residence had convinced Penny that her virginity was something she should be trying to get rid of, preferably without fanfare, blood, or hysterics, but Al insisted on treating it as something very precious. We should wait, he said. For what? she wondered. Until we're married? As if she would ever marry someone like Al.

I want you, she whispered one afternoon, yet so faintly he had to ask, What did you say? And then she couldn't say it. Later, she woke to heavy breathing beside her on the bed and realized he was jerking off, his back slick with sweat, which left her limp with desire. Other times, she shrank from him. If he took off his shirt in the backyard and then tried to kiss her, she immediately felt disgusted by his damp chest, the black hairs above his belt buckle, his nose's crater-like pores. This, she decided, was because he wasn't her type. She preferred slimmer builds, finer features. Clever, sarcastic, complicated guys, like Neil Hanson, who had run into her a couple of times in Brandy's and asked all about U of T, seeming even a little jealous of that guy she was sometimes with. (Oh, that's just Al, she'd said without elaborating.)

Just like a real couple, she and Al had their weekly date nights: Thursday and Friday in Brandy's Lounge, where they'd first met, and Tuesday at the Grawood, which showed old movies on a TV mounted above the bar. They watched *Citizen Kane*, *The Way We Were*, Bruce Lee's *The Way of the Dragon* (during the fight scenes, Al kept murmuring, Decent), and *Blue Hawaii* with Elvis Presley. Al considered the King a much better singer than her geeky Elvis Costello. Elvis Presley is the geeky one, she complained, and he got so fat. Al's response was to hum her the opening bars of "Can't Help Falling in Love."

He always wanted to get to the student pub before the movie started so they could talk, though he rarely said all that much himself. After a few beers, mind you, he might start reminiscing about his childhood. He'd been small for his age and so afraid of the barber, a middle-aged Greek who never smiled, that at one point his hair got as long as a girl's. Once at the pool, the other boys insisted that he was a girl and kicked him out of the changing room. His mom marched him right back in and yanked his pants down. See! she'd said. Oh, that must have been so traumatic, Penny remarked, but Al seemed to find the story funny. He never criticized other people the way she did, gently rebuking her when she put down old high school friends or called her divorced father a drunk.

If she went suddenly quiet, he always wanted to know what she was thinking about. Nothing, she'd say because it was usually something disloyal. The one time she asked him this, he gave her such a hound-dog look that she immediately wished she hadn't. You, he said.

No wonder going out with the girls was such a relief. The night Neil Hanson came on to her, Al was supposed to be on a fishing trip with a friend. Handsome, as she and her girlfriends called Neil, had barely noticed her in high school, but now that they were both going to universities in Upper Canada, he couldn't leave her alone, whispering that he'd been a fool back then and she was deep, he could tell. That night, he kept urging her to ditch the others and go for a walk so that they could really talk, and on a bench facing the harbour, he confessed that he'd liked her all summer. Also that he was full of bullshit and that sometimes he didn't know who was talking, his true self or the bullshit. Then he started necking with her while at the same time deftly unsnapping her jeans. She managed to stop him from putting his hand down, though they did neck some more. He also wrote her number on a liquor store receipt, getting her to spell out her last name. Nothing, she told herself, really happened. Yet the kissing worried her, especially as Al had called just before she left with the girls for the bars. His fishing friend never picked him up, so he was sitting at home drinking his case of Moosehead with his mom. Penny didn't suggest he come out with them, but Nance ran into him later in Brandy's, looking, she reported the next day, very drunk and sad.

On her last night in Halifax, Al insisted on taking her out to dinner. At the restaurant, a new seafood place near the waterfront that she wondered how he could possibly afford, he ordered a carafe of wine and immediately downed the taster glass the waitress poured him, which would have embarrassed her more if it hadn't been only the house red. He also ate both their sprigs of parsley. When she said, It's just for decoration, he exaggerated his chewing. She thought he looked silly in his beige corduroy blazer and glanced away when he ordered a third carafe. He kept telling her how much he was going to miss her. Guess we'll have to make do with writing letters, he said. He also told her he liked her because she was different, which irritated her even more because he knew only the old Penny, the one she was trying so hard in Toronto to get rid of. She and Neil Hanson had talked about this: how no one from here seemed to get how much they'd changed.

Naturally, they ran into Neil in Brandy's. Penny had already drunk two Singapore Slings in addition to all that wine at dinner, so certain details would remain fuzzy. She remembered Neil squeezing next to her in the booth and asking when she was going back to Toronto. Bet you can't wait, he'd said, ignoring Al. He must have also asked for her residence address so he could visit, because she wrote it down for him on a napkin. (His ballpoint pen was almost dry, so she had to do this twice. The first napkin ripped.) He definitely ran a hand up along her thigh under her dress. But she was sure she'd stopped him when his fingers reached her underpants.

In the cab going home, she almost threw up (she'd remember the driver fretting about his upholstery and

Al telling him to shove it) but in the doorway of her father's house felt suddenly so horny that she seized Al by the belt. They necked against the radiator box and fell twice going up the stairs. She could tell he was angry, but that seemed to only excite them both more. Aiming for her bed, they fell again, landing hard on the carpet, and the last sensation she would remember was Al's belt buckle grinding against her abdomen as a pile of her records toppled backward behind her head.

When she woke, he was gone, and she was lying on her bed under the covers. Her first thought was they must have finally done it, but then she noticed she was still fully dressed.

IN TORONTO, PENNY MOSTLY FORGOT ABOUT AL. He did send her a letter, as promised. In her college mailroom, she'd thought for a moment it might be from Neil, which made his plodding description of vocational school, the childlike handwriting and misspelling of university, even more grating. *Love Albert (Foley)*, he wrote. She didn't write him back. She was busy with essays, and what could she have said anyway? It had been nothing but a summer fling. One that ended badly. Yet a month or so later, when she had intercourse for the first time (Neil finally found that napkin), she couldn't help wondering if her small sense of deflation— not to mention the lack of any real feeling (it had been very quick, which afterward he suggested was a compliment)—might not be connected in some obscure way to Al. Maybe she had been hoping for some fanfare.

Of course, forgetting would have been a lot easier if her father hadn't kept mentioning him on the phone. Al was still dropping by the house. He and her father would watch TV together. Sometimes, he'd do small jobs: rake leaves, hose down the patio. I hope you're not telling him things about me, Penny warned, and another time, I don't get it, what on earth do you two have in common? After that, her father grew more reticent. He did tell her about Tammy. No doubt he thought she would be relieved to hear that Al had a new girlfriend. And she was, though a little surprised, Tammy being so much younger and it all seeming to happen so quickly. Al, I told him, you need to get out more, her father reported. Don't worry about me, go have some fun. And apparently that very night he'd taken a cab to Brandy's and there she'd been, waiting by the pay phones.

They got engaged that next summer and were married two years later. By this time, Penny was finished her BA and dating a law student with baby-fine blond hair and clothes considerably nicer than her own, so when her father asked if she'd mind his going to the wedding, she merely groaned. Why are you even asking me that? Afterward, though, she couldn't help quizzing him a little. One of Al's brothers apparently got quite drunk at the reception and made an off-colour speech, but the rest of the Foley family were very nice, her father said, and the bride pretty if on the short side. Al was working as an electrician now and Tammy had started secretarial school. Their plan was to move in with his parents and save for a house on the same street. It all sounded so Halifax.

The relationship with the law student didn't last. Nor did her marriage in the early nineties to an up-and-coming novelist who cheated on her with his agent. These men knew her as Penelope. She was executive director now of a small magazine association (executive dogsbody, she liked to say) and, after her divorce, the sole owner of a narrow townhouse in Parkdale. She still dated. She wasn't completely soured on men. Not that she believed in Mr Right or that a woman necessarily needed a family of her own to feel fulfilled (she wasn't sure she even wanted children). Rather that since her early twenties, she'd simply never lost faith that someone new was around the corner. You just have to keep putting yourself out there, she told her single Toronto friends, joking that she couldn't go into Loblaws without running into some guy in the cereal aisle she'd slept with once, usually in the company of his wife and new baby. Her high school friends, most of them married now with preteen kids (except for Nance thankfully), wouldn't have found this as funny. She suspected they pitied her from their palatial family rooms, which rankled her more than she cared to admit.

From time to time, she thought of Al, especially after a stupid fling with Neil in her forties. She'd run into Handsome at Nancy's wedding. They'd commiserated about being the only two single people left in the whole wide world, then slipped back to her hotel room, and for almost three years, he called her whenever he happened to be in Toronto on business. Naturally, he'd broken things off to marry a twenty-six-year-old actress. When he called to explain he wouldn't be calling anymore, he said that he knew she'd understand. They'd never been that serious and she was not the sentimental type. Around then, it occurred to Penny that she'd been a fool to ever think Neil and his ilk were her type. Al had been different. She remembered how completely he'd rushed in. Tell me if you want me to go, he would say during those long afternoons in her father's house, and when she shrugged—Whenever—he'd tease, Careful, Penny, or I might just stay forever.

She wasn't really that surprised when he turned up at her father's funeral. He'd already sent a card. One of those old-fashioned religious cards with a photo of a Celtic cross and a reading inside from John: *I will not leave you comfortless, I will come to you.* Below this, Al had written, in the same childlike rounded hand she recognized from her college mailroom a quarter century ago, *Dear Penny, I'm so sorry for your loss, I will always remember your dad's kindness to me.* Her father, of course, had merely been lonely. But Al always saw the best in people: it was one of the qualities that had most infuriated her at twenty.

In the church, she'd kept glancing behind her, to see if he *would* indeed come as the card said. And suddenly there he was in the foyer, wearing a tight blue suit and looking stockier than he'd been at twenty-two yet not fat (she'd always thought he would get fat, like Elvis).

He slid into one of the last pews and kneeled to do a sign of the cross (he was a Catholic, she remembered) before sitting back and studying his leaflet. He didn't look up, but she felt sure he'd seen her. And he was alone, which sent a tiny thrill through her. When she stood to deliver her eulogy, she could feel his eyes on her and was glad she'd splurged on a new black dress from Holt's, discounted but still more than she could really afford. My father would have been so happy to see you all here, she said from the pulpit, gazing only at Al.

Confident they would speak at the reception, she took her time entering the church hall, greeting a few old family friends, chatting to the minister about Toronto housing prices. Once she had a cup of tea in her hands, she scanned the tables of sweets, the clutch of people gathered around the photo boards she'd carefully constructed, the lines for coffee and tea. No Al. Maybe he'd stepped out to the washroom. She waited cradling her cold tea longer than made sense.

IN THE YEARS THAT FOLLOWED, PENNY WOULD sometimes stumble across names of men she'd dated in her twenties and thirties and marvel at how few she could even picture anymore. With social media, she supposed, this kind of forgetting must be more difficult, the faces of old boyfriends just a click away. Also, they'd taken fewer photos. She didn't have a single one of Al and had tossed his one letter into the waste bin the same day she opened it. Even the condolence card was long gone. She didn't remember everything: mostly just how smitten he'd been and this humbling sense that she'd made a mistake, taken a wrong turn or thought there'd be more turns. Over time, his name acquired an almost karmic significance, if only because it stuck with her, all lit up in her mind like a neon question mark, when so many others hadn't. Al Foley, she would say to herself sometimes, apropos of nothing.

One Friday night, shortly before her fifty-fifth birthday, she found herself tearing up over an Elvis greatest-hits CD in a Value Village bargain bin. After she got home, she opened a bottle of red wine and searched for him on Facebook. The only two Albert Foleys she found were a FedEx employee in Detroit and a beefy-looking young man in a white tuxedo from Waterloo. She tried tapping his name and *Halifax* into Google. Three A. Foleys popped up, but the two with addresses didn't live on or anywhere near Pepperell. She acknowledged that it was possible he and Tammy had not in the end bought a house on the same street as his parents but couldn't picture herself calling up perfect strangers: Are you the Al Foley who dated a Penny Simon in the early eighties? Even if she were to call the right one, what could she say? And what if Tammy answered? It struck her then just how much she'd always relied on Al to be there, by which she meant in Halifax, on Pepperell Street. And more foolish still, to be there *for* her.

Naturally, she couldn't help then going over that terrible night again in her mind. How she'd let Neil feel her up in the bar, how silently furious Al had been, and in the morning how she'd blithely assumed he'd taken advantage of her drunkenness. Only now she remembered something else. That hadn't been the end. Shortly before noon the next day, he'd appeared at her front door, hair still dripping from his shower, Boston Bruins T-shirt stuck to his chest. Why? To help her pack up her stereo as he'd promised. Oh, right, she'd said, as if it made no difference to her whether she saw him one last time. Al, for once, didn't kiss her, instead heading straight to the living room and unplugging all the cords. He also boxed up the records spilled over on her bedroom floor, placing *My Aim Is True* on top. Then he waited with her on the porch for her father to come home from the office and drive her to the airport. All Penny could think about was that cocktail napkin with her address scrawled on it that Neil had crunched into a front pocket of his jeans. She hoped it wouldn't fall out somehow or dissolve in the wash. When Al at last leaned in, she tweaked his nose. He tried to match her tone, scooped up the cat (Kiss Penny good-bye for me), though his brown eyes stayed serious and remained that way she sensed long after she stopped bothering to look back from the car. And she'd thrown away his letter, had stood in a church hall expecting him to come to her.

Later, she would wonder why it took her so long to google Tammy. That was where she found him, below the black-and-white photo of a smiling, plump-faced woman with bobbed light hair: *Survived by her loving husband of twenty-eight years, Albert Foley, of Waterloo.* Their children were listed too, Candice and Albert Junior

(Dawn), along with two granddaughters, Sophia and Emma. Tammy had worked for the Waterloo Catholic District School Board as a secretary. She had been a Girl Guide leader, an alto in the church choir, an adoring grandma. Donations could be made to the Grand River Regional Cancer Centre. She'd been just forty-eight. So young. So sad. Yet how to stop or deny the hopeful tributary this news opened up inside her. All this time, he'd been only an hour and a half away.

Penny waited until she felt more sober before sending him a message care of the funeral home. Just to let him know that she'd heard about Tammy and how sorry she was, adding that she was still in Toronto. Al emailed the next day.

ON THE DRIVE TO WATERLOO, SHE FELT AS IF everything in her field of vision had become simultaneously blurred and sharpened: her hands on the steering wheel, cars darting in and out of the lane, the broken CD case open on the seat beside her. Each of Al's emails over the past three weeks had brought a sharp ping of pleasure. And now that they were actually meeting—Al's idea, a family-style diner where they could have coffee and a bite to eat—she'd entered a state of what, although she was not spiritual, she could only call bliss. She'd felt like this before, of course. With other men, with Neil even. But she didn't want to dwell on past mistakes. The point was that she was feeling like this again, and all because of Al.

He'd done well, owned his own company with four employees—take that, she told her twenty-year-old self. He and Tammy had also travelled, mostly to Florida but after her first round of chemo to London and Paris. Candice was engaged, and Al Junior (the white-tuxedoed youth on Facebook)'s twin girls were now four. They touched on the summer of 1982 only lightly, Penny suggesting that she'd treated him badly and Al saying, no, she shouldn't think that, that he had no regrets. But she knew they were both thinking about it.

Several of her friends had reconnected with old boyfriends over Facebook, and while once she might have been tempted to roll her eyes, she couldn't help but feel these reclaimed teenage romances were likely truer than the algorithmic matches engineered on EliteSingles or eHarmony. Surely some things in life were simply meant to be.

Navigating the streets of downtown Waterloo, though, she couldn't help also worrying about her flyaway hair that no amount of straightening controlled anymore, the wine belly she was trying to camouflage with her oversized swing tunic. In the parking lot of Jack's Family Restaurant, she averted her glance from the overnight bag she'd stowed (just in case) in the backseat. He, of all people, would recognize how much she'd changed.

But he'd changed too. Glancing down the length of the restaurant, she immediately spotted the one middle-aged man sitting in a booth alone and thought, oh, there he is. Then, experiencing a sudden double take, maybe not. Only when Al half rose could she be sure. He *was* a little fat now. When he put his arms around her, though, she decided that the extra padding was reassuring, making her feel more relaxed about her own. The brown eyes, the impossibly long lashes were the same, yet she'd forgotten how gruff his voice was.

"Penny Simon. Beautiful as ever."

She heard herself laugh. "You look good too, Al. The years have been kind to you."

Even before he lowered his gaze, she wished she could take back *kind*.

"Well, we should get you a coffee," he said, glancing nervously about.

He hadn't touched his own, despite his side of the table being scattered with empty creamers and spilt sugar packets, and for a moment, she despaired. They were too old for this. But once Al was able to catch the waitress's attention and Penny had foolishly ordered a latte instead of a regular coffee and managed her first bitter sips, she tried the same approach as she had over email, asking him questions. He'd become quite a good talker, she noted with amused affection. And as he told her about his mother's colon cancer (they'd covered the details of Tammy's breast cancer by email) and the trouble they'd all had with his eldest brother (drug addiction, constant requests for money, a restraining order) and how adorable his granddaughters were, Penny basked in his nearness, remembering those long afternoons in her father's house and how she used to sit on his lap and he would caress her face and hair. How odd that it had taken her this long, almost her whole life, to realize that she loved him.

When he ran out of words, she wished she had the courage to reach across the table and touch the large blunt hand lying open beside his cup. Then suddenly his eyes were wet, and she *was* touching it.

"Penny, I'm sorry."

"Don't be," she said. As she caressed his wrist, she heard in her head the same song he'd hummed all those years ago in the Grawood and that she'd played over and over on YouTube while crafting her emails to him.

"It's just—"

She stroked his fingers. "It's okay. I'm sorry too," she said, adding so quietly she wasn't sure he even heard, "Al, darling."

When he looked at her this time, his whole face glistened. So raw and powerful was his emotion, so bared for all to see, that for an instant she faltered.

"It's just—" he repeated, piercing her with those soft brown eyes. "I know that this might sound corny to you. But she was the love of my life."

ON THE DRIVE BACK INTO TORONTO, SHE STOPPED at the Dundas West Loblaws, settling on a plastic triangle of blue cheese, an overpriced box of gourmet crackers, and a twelve-dollar bottle of California Merlot. Once she got home, she tossed the overnight bag on the couch and flicked on the big overhead light, then stood at the kitchen counter and poured her first drink. At least she hadn't acted like a complete fool. Thanks for listening to all my troubles, he'd said after he walked her to her car, giving her then another friendly hug. She ripped open the cracker box and its inner pouch with her fingers but had to use a knife for the cheese container. What had she been thinking? That Tammy was some sort of consolation prize? She really needed to cut back on the wine. She was starting to get maudlin.

But that wasn't it, not all of it. The barb dug deeper. She thought of his face before he put into words what she should have known all along, its fierce, almost rapturous clarity. How she couldn't help but look away.

So it goes.

Went.

More Merlot splashing into her glass.

Pomegranate

THE AFRICAN GIRLS LINK ARMS. TOGETHER, THEY lift their knees. Jump one way, then the other, whirl their bright red dresses. Their teeth are like fresh chalk lined up in a box. See us, they seem to say through these white, white teeth. We have nothing to eat but bug-infested porridge that we grind ourselves with sticks on the parched dirt, but we are happy, sooo happy.

Now the camera jerks back and pans the row of people watching: men in pale slacks and loose white shirts, Kodak Brownies slung around their necks, a woman wearing cat's-eye sunglasses and pearls.

"Christ," Tina says. "Doesn't she know what fucking year it is?"

The rest of us say nothing. That's because Sister MacNamara is staring at our table, a finger pressed to her skinny lips, even though the movie has no sound.

We know what she wants. She wants us to imagine what it would be like to be truly hungry so we can become more like the grateful dancing African girls. No stinky egg-salad or leftover-party-platter-cold-cut sandwiches for us today. No carrot sticks mummified in Saran, no miniature tins of Del Monte fruit cocktail. No bites of Mona's mother's chocolate cake. Instead, Sister MacNamara has doled out bowls of watered-down Campbell's tomato soup with single-serving packages of soda crackers, the kind that come on the plate with the roll at the Gag and Spew.

At the table in front of ours, Patty Moore lifts each spoonful to her lips like it's the blood of Christ. She hasn't even touched her crackers. The little cellophane cube sits primly beside her water cup, as if she isn't going to just stuff her face full of candy from the Little General the second the hunger meal is over. We've seen her at her locker when she thinks no one's looking, her cheeks bulging like a squirrel's.

We're not fat, not like Patty. Yet even on Sister Mac-Namara's starvation diet, we can feel our legs beginning to swell. We don't need some stupid tourist movie from the fifties to teach us about hunger. It won't leave us alone, taking us at our desks and lockers, when we're riding the city bus, every time we pass the Little General or the snack drawer at home with its open bag of Hickory Sticks, and we worry constantly. Our calves are safely encased in navy knee socks, but our thighs, our thighs under our kilts are bare, nothing to hold them in.

POMEGRANATE

"We should just go." Tina glares through those limp brown bangs she hasn't cut since Greaser Day. "What's she going to do? Tell our mothers?"

We hate the headmistress just as much as she does. The way Sister MacNamara marches into the study hall in her pink tweed suit and matching pumps with the tiny black bows. Drawing back the curtains to let the sun shine in. Getting Patty to read out loud her barfy poetry (*Beneath the draping strawberry green lurked a beagle, he looked mean*). And now these ridiculous hunger meals, as if she thinks every girl in the upper school wants to become a missionary in Africa, when all *we* want is to slow-dance with the Gorsebrook boys again. But we're not crazy. Not like Tina, who laughed openly in the study hall at Patty's poem. And when Sister MacNamara told her, You don't know what you are inside but God does, rolled her eyes and said in front of all the girls, You're right, I *don't* know what I am inside.

"Let's just go." Tina scrapes her chair back hard.

Still, we say nothing. Mona isn't finished all her soup, and we won't go anywhere without her.

We don't just want to be near her, we want to *be* her, to look down at our legs under the lunchroom table and see hers. But Tina never lets us get too near. And ever since Greaser Day, she won't stop touching her. Twirling a finger through that perfectly flat hair. Whispering in her ear, Hey babe, as if Mona's still her girlfriend for the day. What a cute couple, the older girls all cooed. And Mona did look cute in her mother's poodle skirt and a pair of frilly white ankle socks. But we didn't like to look at Tina on Greaser Day. She'd cut her hair around a kitchen bowl the night before, then slicked it back in the morning with Vaseline and showed up at school wearing her mother's boyfriend's undershirt, an empty cigarette pack stuffed up one sleeve (we know the pack was empty because Sister MacNamara made her open it) and a thumb hooked through the belt loop of her Levi's jeans. When she and Mona paraded down the hall at lunch, Tina looking so happy for a change, we glanced away. The same as when one of the older girls in the locker room suddenly turns and snaps, What are you staring at?

Mona wipes her fingers on her paper napkin. "Okay," she says, giving the napkin a little push off the table. "Let's go."

Tina is first up. Then all we hear is chair legs. Sister MacNamara opens her mouth, one hand clutching the pale green neck of her projector, while the African girls jerk silently across the hanging screen. But we're already out the door. All we needed was a little push. Now we're running. Tina, then Mona, her strawberry-blond hair whirling out behind her. Then the rest of us, laughing, whooping. Even goody-two-shoes Karen. We expect yells, sirens, angry nun faces staring down from the walls, Sister MacNamara dropping out of a ceiling tile. But nothing stops us. And now we're hurling ourselves against the door, spilling out into the bright stillness of the schoolyard. This one perfect moment, our escape from the hunger meal, filling us up like a Sara Lee frozen cake we've been gorging on from the box with our hands.

POMEGRANATE

It doesn't last. The fullness never does. Already our stomachs are turning hard, making us double over in the sunshine. Already Tina is glaring through her bangs. Maybe she's mad that the other grade eights didn't get up, just us. Or wishes she and Mona were stepping out into all that white-hot stillness alone. Karen gets ready to say something, squints through those silver-rimmed glasses that with her round chin and thin blond bangs make her look like a nerdy-girl version of John Denver, and we know it's going to be something stupid, about the litter crisis or aerosol sprays ripping a hole in the ozone layer or how the Russians have a missile that could flatten Montreal. But before she can, Tina slaps her so hard her glasses fly partway off her nose.

ON OUR GOLD-TASSELLED MENUS, CRISSCROSS-ing sticks of bamboo spell out The Garden View, though the only view from our booth is a faded mural of cherry blossoms and even these we like to say make us gag. Usually, we order a single plate of French fries, and the sullen old-man waiter snatches our menus away without a word. But today, since Karen's paying, we ask for the Gag and Spew's lunchtime special of pork egg rolls with fried rice, along with two servings of onion rings, three of French fries, and six large Cokes.

Karen hardly notices. She's too happy telling us about the killer bees. "So there was this scientist in South America who wanted to create these super bees that would make more honey, so he crossed regular bees

153

with African ones, but the African bees were way more aggressive and so he had to keep the super bees in quarantine. And then one night a whole hive escaped."

Tina rolls her eyes. "Oh, no. Escape of the Bumblebees!"

Karen wipes her glasses on her blouse. Without them, her lashes won't stop fluttering. She should really be more careful what she says. We could decide to hate her. Instead, she's always trying to get us alone. Why follow them around? she wants to know. Why do their dirty work? Even your voice, she's said to each of us in turn, is becoming a Tina-and-Mona kind of voice.

"It's true," she's saying now. "And what's so freaky is they attack for no reason. All you have to do is start up a lawn mower or bang a window shut. And it doesn't matter how far or how fast you run. They pick their victims' bodies clean to the bone."

"You're gross," Mona says, leaning out of our booth so she can see better up the aisle.

"Yeah," we agree. "You're such a spaz. We're supposed to be having lunch."

"They could come here. They're already in Texas."

But we're craning our heads to see what Mona's looking at, which turns out to be two long-haired hippie guys smoking at a table by the window.

One has let his hair fan out thick and crinkly on broad shoulders, while the other is thinner with long Peter Fonda sideburns and a greasy ponytail. The thin one is cuter, we decide. Poking out of the ragged cuffs of his jeans are oily dark brown cowboy boots. We're used to seeing hippies at the Public Gardens, girls mostly, selling things. They sit on faded patchwork blankets, their handmade macramé belts and velvet mirror-encrusted shoulder bags looped behind them on the fence, and stare at us through their veils of hair, as if they think we're the freaks.

The two hippie guys haven't glanced over even once, but Mona shifts her bum away from Tina's, pulls her own veil of hair forward, and suddenly they are. Mona must have telepathic powers because they're staring right at her, and maybe it's our imagination but the one we like best winks at her. Mona presses her lips together in a secret smile. And right away we're picturing her on a blanket waiting for her man, and he's the one in the cowboy boots and she's so happy to see him she jumps into his skinny brown arms.

"Christ," Tina says. "Where's our food?" She reaches across Karen, starts slapping the metal accordion pages of the tabletop jukebox.

"Play 'Crocodile Rock,'" we say. "Play 'Leroy Brown.'"

But Mona wants the Wings' "Live and Let Die."

For a moment, we think the jukebox is broken, that Tina's been too rough. Then rising above the clink of knives and coffee cups we hear Paul's voice, singing about our hearts being like an open book, and we sway together on our side of the booth, waiting for the crash of chords. When it comes, we turn and peek up the aisle at those two guys. We keep expecting them to stare again at Mona. She's curving her arms as she sings along with Paul, her straight, straight hair spilling across her face like spaghetti from a box.

We were sure the Gorsebrook boys would also stare. She looked so perfect in her beaded shirt and five-star jeans, her hair brushed so many times it glowed. But it was us they asked to dance. And when the DJ croaked in his raspy smoker's voice, Here's a slow one to hold your baby to real close, even Patty Moore got tapped. We could see her burrowing into the swarm of bodies, the boy's hands cupped on either side of her big bum, while Mona still leaned against the dark gym wall. All Tina's fault. She wouldn't leave her alone all night. But what could we do, our faces crushed against the Gorsebrook boys' flannel chests?

The hippie guys are getting ready to go. They drop their butts into coffee cups, grab their lighters, scatter coins. Surely, they'll look back. For Mona's sake, we sing louder, open our mouths wide as if to swallow her song whole. But the song cuts out before they even reach the door.

AT LEAST OUR LUNCH HAS COME. THE WAITER puts down each plate with a grim flourish. So many plates. We can't believe we ordered all this food. Tina saws through an egg roll with her knife, and its grey innards ooze into the rice.

"Mm-mm," she says. "Almost as good as Campbell's."

We clench our straws with our teeth so the Coke will go down slower. Somehow our glasses still drain. Then there's nothing to do but stab a French fry, and another, bang our palms against the Heinz bottle.

"An-ti-ci-paaa-tion," Tina sneers.

The French fries are mushy, but we eat them anyway. The fried coating slips off the onion rings so we use our fingers. We try not to touch the special because if we start, we know we'll get fat, but then we do, forking up egg-roll intestines and dirty rice so fast we can barely taste them.

In a booth in the back corner, two guys we didn't notice before are lighting up. Their cigarette smoke mixes with the smell rising from our ravaged plates. One of them smiles at us. He has on a silky shirt patterned with wobbly red and orange rings, all these gold chains, while his feathered hair puffs out around his ears like David Cassidy's. When we were younger, we were in love with David and can still remember how his lips felt when we kissed him in a magazine: soft and unresisting, slightly waxy like a leaf. This guy is small like David too, so small that he's almost swallowed up by the cherry-red backing of the corner booth. The other guy is old and bald and wears a satin dressing gown, bruised purple with shiny wide lapels. The little one is cuter, we decide. Much cuter.

"Look at those faggots," Tina says.

We look again. The one who reminded us of David sucks in his cheeks and blows us a perfect smoke ring. The skin around his mouth cracks when he smiles.

"Christ, he's wearing makeup."

"Gross, what a freak!" We can't believe we thought that guy was cute.

"Who the fuck does he think he is?" Tina says.

He waves, and Karen starts to lift her hand.

Tina slaps it down. "Jesus Christ, what are you, a freak too?"

"Who cares?" Mona says.

"Christ, I can't stand looking at him. He's such a fucking freak."

"Then don't." Mona groans, gazing up the aisle again at the empty window table.

Tina picks up a French fry: a pale, cold worm that makes our mouths water, even though we're so full we think we might throw up at any second. She dangles it near the top of Mona's blouse.

Mona tries to swat her hand away.

Tina braces her other arm against the booth and holds the French fry steady.

Mona pushes against her, and we wonder if she'll cry like she used to when she first came in grade five. On our way to lunch, we'd see her: the new girl everyone wanted for her new best friend, sitting on a chair in the headmistress's office, lips clenched tight to try to stop herself. And we wished so hard that Sister MacNamara would tap us in the hall. That she would say, Anne-Marie, or Carol, or Lisa, could you stay with Mona until her mother comes? And we would get to go home with Mona in her mother's sky-blue Cadillac. We wanted so much to be the one she chose, to escape with her into this sunlit other world.

Instead, we just kept walking. Blurred in with all the other girls.

Tina jams the fry down Mona's blouse. Mona grabs Tina's wrist and twists. Her lips are clenched, but not from trying not to cry. The two of them shove and claw each other, push Karen up against the corner of the jukebox. We wish now we were back at school—in the study hall, the locker room, even the lunchroom with the dancing African girls. If only the Gorsebrook boys were here. We would fly into their arms. We are so ready, want so much to bury our faces in hot flannel and feel their muffled heartbeats on our cheeks.

"Just leave me the fuck alone," Mona says so loud even the waiter on his barstool looks around.

Tina mashes the fry into a ball, then tosses it into Karen's glass where it expands like a time-lapse pupa we watched once in a movie in science class. "Look," she says. "A killer bee."

That's when David Cassidy slides out of the corner booth. Maybe it's the psychedelic shirt, more like a blouse, unbuttoned nearly to his belly button, or the way he rises on his toes, but he scares us coming up the aisle. His red pants are so tight we can see his bulge.

"Are you convent girls?" He has a funny baby voice.

"What was your first clue?" Tina says.

"My sister was a convent girl."

"Oh, really? *Was* she?"

"Yes!" he exclaims. "She wore a light blue blouse, just like yours, but her shoes were brown, not black. Sometimes, she let me help her polish them with a special cloth. I was just a little boy then. She was my big sister. She loved the nuns. She wanted to be a nun when she grew up."

"No kidding. Did she want to be a missionary too and go to Africa?"

"Oh, she would have loved that. She talked about the children in Africa a lot."

"Yes, we do that too. Poor kiddies." Tina grins, and we see now that he's the one who should be scared.

But Karen naturally has to open her big fat mouth. "What happened to your sister?"

"She got married. She has two little boys of her own now."

Tina tosses us an eye roll. "So, she didn't fulfill her girlhood dream and become a nun and go to Africa?"

He looks confused. "No."

"Is she sad about that?" Karen asks. "Does she wish she did?"

"No. I don't know. I don't think so. I don't see her anymore."

He glances back at his friend in the purple dressing gown, then places a hand on top of Tina's. "You girls are all so beautiful. So innocent. I just wanted to tell you that."

"If you say so," Tina says.

And we don't dare look up in case we crack up.

After he's gone, she keeps scratching the back of her wrist. "Fucking freak."

"Yeah, what a total freak," we say.

Mona sighs. "Let's just get out of here."

And we're up, patting down our pleats and gliding up the aisle past the grease-stained cherry blossoms—when Tina flicks her bangs. "I'm going to go back there and tell them what we really think of them."

"What *is* your problem?" Mona says.

And Karen pleads, "No. Please. Don't. Please."

But Tina's already marching to their booth, and our stomachs clench. We want to throw up. We want to laugh our heads off. We can't believe she's doing this. We watch her slip in next to him on the vinyl seat. *So* innocent. Watch her cup her hands against his blow-dried hair while the guy in the dressing gown looks on like God. Then we can't stand it anymore. All we want now is to get rid of the chalk taste in our mouths. We turn to Karen, her fingers fluttering as she hands over our bill. Watch as the Chinese waiter studies blankly the number circled with his own pen, Mona already pushing on the bright red door, letting in a ladleful of air. Only when we can hear Tina's panting at our necks do we dare look back, and then just long enough to glimpse his sunken baby-face.

WE'RE RUNNING AGAIN, DODGING SHOPPERS and parking meters, our Oxfords thumping like our hearts, which are not open books but a teeming hive we guard even from ourselves. We stop just once, at the Little General, where Tina spends the rest of Karen's money on Hostess potato chips and Oh Henry! bars, a paper bag of penny caramels, and, because Mona wants one, a dusty pomegranate from a wooden crate. Then we keep on running until we reach the Gardens, ducking past the woven belts and mirrored bags, the emaciated girls on their hippie blankets, and collapsing finally on the hard-packed dirt behind the fence. We're hungry again, so, sooo hungry. Everything we ate, the French fries and onion rings, the cracker crumbs we licked off our palms at Sister MacNamara's hunger meal dissolving like a dream. This time, we don't hold back. We tear apart chip bags, chew the foil off chocolate bars, cram caramels down our throats, try to stop up all the hollow spaces we know the Gorsebrook boys—even as we still long for them to feel us up—can never satisfy. Tina cracks open the pomegranate on a pointed rock. Its seeds smile up at us like bright red teeth. She offers one half to Mona, and the rest of us swarm over the other, ripping out its parched flesh, bloodying our lips and chins.

Bundle of Joy

"AND THE LAST THING THEY NEED IS ANOTHER dog," Ruth said, but Joe didn't even glance this time, just crossed into the exit lane.

When he took the ramp a little fast, she braced her neck against the headrest, feeling the gift bag at her feet tip. It was bright yellow with a turquoise felt elephant glued to each side and a matching card on which Ruth had written—because Joe was rushing her and she couldn't think of anything more original—*For Our Little Bundle of Joy*.

They were going to see their grandson. A proper visit, not like that first day in hospital when Erin had only cared about getting an awkward photo or two on Devin's iPhone. Ruth didn't even have time to take her coat off. Afterward, sitting in the dreary coffee shop, she commented that the baby had short legs and Joe raged,

For Christ's sake, Ruth, he's a baby. Why are you so negative? I'm not, she'd said.

But what was the point in trying to explain?

She knew they talked about her. During Erin's middle and high school years, when the simplest observation about clothing or study habits got automatically misconstrued as judgment, Ruth would often hear Joe whispering at her bedroom door: Your mom means well, or You're right, she shouldn't have said that. More recently, she'd begun to suspect Erin called him at the office. How else to explain all the little things he knew that she didn't? And none of Erin's choices ever seemed to disappoint him. When she gave up the idea of medical school, he merely murmured something about finding one's passion, leaving it to Ruth to ask the difficult questions at Thanksgiving. And when she moved in with Maureen, he acted as if his only child taking up with her married English professor was exactly what he'd been hoping for all along.

Joe had also seen nothing remarkable in Erin's about-face when the relationship with Maureen unravelled: the unremarkable data-analyst boyfriend, her pregnancy at thirty-four after insisting for so long that they could forget about grandchildren, and now a house in the suburbs. It's all good, he said, which really should be his epitaph. And when Ruth dared suggest that all this newfound conformity might be yet another attempt to shock them, he'd groaned. You know not everything is about you, Ruth.

She managed at least to keep her mouth shut while passing all the usual car dealerships and a mammoth Costco. Her husband didn't share her horror of suburbia, not anymore. He was bent forward, cradling the steering wheel as if all the near-identical flat beige duplexes belonged to Erin and he needed to shield them from her mother's scorn. It was not a new or particularly fashionable subdivision but close apparently to Devin's workplace as well as a large dog park, presumably the muddy crater appearing now beyond Joe's hunched shoulders. She wondered if this was where Erin would take Noah for walks in the fancy jogging stroller they'd paid for. She couldn't see a sidewalk anywhere. Most of the streets, named inexplicably after the great cities of Europe, were like mini-expressways, ridged with stubborn snow as hard and black as basalt.

When he turned at last onto Amsterdam Court and she spotted the duplex Erin had described as four in, Ruth found herself hoping foolishly that theirs would be the side with the burlap-covered bushes and recently painted window boxes. If it was, she could bring them flats of annuals in June—begonias, lobelia, and sweet potato vine—and maybe in the fall tulip bulbs to complement the Netherlands theme. But naturally theirs was the side she'd been trying not to look at, with the cracked concrete stoop and nothing out front but a single scrawny blue spruce, its top branches already dead.

"We're here," Joe said.

If she were a different sort of wife, a better sort, Ruth might have reached across the armrest and patted his thigh, dissipating for a moment the fresh tension that had accumulated between them on the drive. Instead, she stared stonily at her daughter's stark new home.

Beige brick like all the rest, and about as inviting as a bank. Surely she'd heard the car and would come to the door, ease her father's nervousness about the weekend, and Ruth's too, wave and call out to them. Or at least get Devin to come. If she did, everything would be okay. They would hug on the cracked stoop, and Devin would offer Joe a beer, and Ruth would be forgiven for that thing she'd said last summer after too much wine and get to hold her grandson for longer than a photo.

But no one came.

Ruth reached for the gift bag with its crown of turquoise tissue paper and rested it on her lap while Joe got out to fetch their overnight bags, slamming the trunk with more of the same anxious cheer.

"All right, let's go, Ruth," he said, opening the passenger door for her.

But she felt the same as she did increasingly when she first woke up. Especially if she'd drunk more than two glasses the night before. Joe would be in the shower, and she'd think, Okay, I need to get up now, before the water stops, before he comes into the room and starts putting on his briefs, turns on the CBC. Except it was as if she were being held down by all these invisible tiny pins.

"Ruth?"

She wrenched her legs around. "Coming."

It had begun to rain, one of those sloppy, cold March showers, and although she held the gift bag close to her coat, a fat drop landed on the tissue paper. Joe had to ring twice, and Ruth couldn't help herself.

"Finally."

"Nice to see you too, Mom," Erin said.

Her fine brown hair had been raked into a stubby ponytail, and her complexion, usually so clear and smooth, was blotchy, the way it used to get in elementary school when almost anything—trying on new clothes at the mall, a careless word—could inflame it. For a second, Ruth wondered if she and Joe had come on the wrong weekend. But Joe was already reaching forward, kissing Erin clumsily on the nose.

One whole wall of the extremely narrow entrance was taken up with a mirrored closet, so Ruth had no choice except to stare at her sagging chin and neck as she pulled off her boots. The closet, predictably, was stuffed with Devin and Erin's junk.

"Where do you want us to put our coats?"

"Shh, could you keep your voice down? He's sleeping."

"We can't wait to see him," Joe whispered, lifting the overnight bags out of the entranceway with exaggerated care and laying his parka overtop.

"Well, like I said, he's sleeping," Erin repeated. Then apparently remembering which parent she was speaking to, "Do you want something, Dad? Water? Tea?"

"No, no, don't trouble yourself," he said, reaching underneath the parka to unzip his bag and removing the two bottles of nice Australian Chardonnay they'd brought. "For later."

"I'm not really drinking wine," Erin said. "But Devin might want some."

"Where is Devin?" Ruth asked more sharply than she intended.

"Out with Asher and Luna."

Asher must be the new one. Ruth couldn't believe they would bring a rescue dog into a house with a five-week-old baby. It also irked her that Devin would take the dogs out just when his in-laws were expected. Or that Erin hadn't thought to offer her father a beer after his long drive.

"I need to use the washroom," she announced.

With her good wool coat bunched up behind her on the toilet seat and the waistband of her black tights digging into her thighs, Ruth felt the inertia from the car return. What was the point in going out there? It would be the same as always. No matter how hard she tried to keep her mouth shut, she'd say something that offended and there'd be a scene, with Joe playing peacemaker but really on Erin's side. And then she'd lie awake all night not knowing what time it was or when she should go into the kitchen, whether there'd be coffee or if she and Joe would have to make their own. Checking the expiry date on the cream, digging through the freezer for bread and the dishwasher for a knife. And Erin, when she finally got up, would act as if there was nothing wrong with this, that to make breakfast for your guests, to make any kind of effort, was old-fashioned, fussy, like throwing dinner parties or dressing up for family.

Joe was right: she was negative.

She could hear him making cooing noises, so Noah must have woken after all. Staring at the gift bag wedged between her calves, she tried to summon the pleasure she'd felt knitting the little blue cardigan inside, how after each row she pressed the soft merino wool against her cheek. But all she could think about was the tissue paper, all crushed from the rain.

PLACING HER COAT ALONGSIDE JOE'S AND FOL-lowing the sound of cooing, she went over in her mind the internet's rules for shutting up. Don't forget, she told herself, they've only just moved in and have a new baby, and two dogs. For that was one of them: *Be kind.*

The main living space, however, struck her as so cheerless, so lacking in comfort or any attempt at beauty, that all she could do was drop the yellow gift bag next to Erin where she sat nursing Noah on the oversized leather couch from Devin's apartment.

"Brought you something."

It was one of those open concept living spaces where everything except the kitchen feels like a waiting area, an impression not helped by the absence of pictures or plants or any knickknacks except for a collection of cords, cables, and remotes on a coffee table that appeared to have been banged together from pallets. The only seats other than the leather couch were two scratched-up wooden office chairs that Devin had explained reverently last summer were mid-century, and Ruth knew by the way Joe kept leaning forward to say, What a cutie, that his back was killing him.

But what bothered her most was how everything to do with Noah was just scattered about the floor. Minia-ture sleepers and onesies, a vinyl change pad and open tin of diaper cream, a brand-new Lamaze caterpillar all mingling together with torn-apart cardboard and plastic packaging and twists of wire and great tufts of dog hair. She remembered after Erin's birth, when she could barely stand, cutting up fresh peaches to put in muffins for visitors and feeling guilty that she hadn't had a chance to vacuum.

When she knelt to screw the top back on the diaper cream, though, Erin only snapped, "You don't have to do that, Mom."

DEVIN DIDN'T GET BACK UNTIL NEARLY SIX, BY which time even Joe seemed to have run out of banal refrains. The dogs entered first. The new one, Asher, knocking up against Luna, Erin's golden Lab from her Maureen years, and then stepping on a baby blanket.

"Asher," Erin crooned. "Come to Mama."

The black-and-white mutt scrambled up onto the couch and promptly stuck its snout into the yellow gift bag. It would have slobbered all over the little cardigan if Joe hadn't swivelled forward in his office chair and gingerly pulled the bag away by its ribbon handle.

Now he sat dangling it between his legs, waiting for their daughter's partner to say hello.

Devin switched on the overhead light, then bent to kiss the top of Erin's ponytail. He was wearing a red-plaid shirt and baggy cuffed jeans, as if he'd just come in from chopping firewood, not watching a bunch of dogs defecate. His beard reminded Ruth of a neglected box hedge. "How's the boy?"

"Well, he's sucking me dry. And you should have seen the giant poop he did."

"Did you do a giant poop, bud? Want me to take him, hon?"

"Yes, please."

"Okay, let me put the dogs away." Devin nudged Asher off the couch, then grabbed both animals by their collars.

"Good to see you, Joe," he said at last. "Ruth."

"We're so happy to be here." Joe placed the gift bag on the floor so that he could reach out his hand, but Devin was busy prodding the dogs into their crates, and now he was lifting Noah out of Erin's arms. "This is such a great place you've found." Joe beamed at the featureless living space. "And what a cutie that Noah is."

"He sure is," Devin said, bouncing him a little roughly in Ruth's opinion. "Would you like a beer, Joe?"

"Only if you're having one."

"I don't think I will," Devin said. "I think I'll just have wine with dinner."

"Oh well. I'm okay then."

"No, I'll get you one. Just give me a sec."

Ruth hoisted herself out of her office chair. "Let me hold Noah for you."

"It's okay. I've got this, Ruth."

But when Devin reached the fridge, instead of a beer, he handed Joe their grandson.

"Aren't you a little cutie?" Joe said.

"That's your Grampy," Erin cooed from the couch.

At the far end of the living space, a sliding door opened onto a cramped deck. Ruth could tell the deck was cramped because no dining-room table blocked her view, just the two crates and a nickel-plated ceiling fan. If Erin had wanted, she could have had the pine table Ruth brought out for overflow at parties or the Victorian wingback from the guest room. But she'd made it clear at Devin's apartment. Her mother's things were dated. Too brown. Well, no kidding, Ruth had replied. They're antiques. The dogs whimpered as she drifted past their crates toward the deck. Her family, immersed in Joe's second time holding Noah, took no notice. A privacy fence, a good eight feet and stained an oppressive clay red, marked out the perimeter of the yard. In one corner, she saw an old wooden doghouse, its white paint mostly peeled off and surrounding it on the yellowed grass all these tubular deposits of dirt. These were everywhere, she realized, and for a moment wondered if Devin and Erin might have aerated before the frost. But there didn't appear to be any corresponding holes in the lawn, just the plugs themselves.

"What are those tube-y things on your grass?" she called out.

Erin and Devin exchanged a glance. "What are you looking at, Ruth?" Devin asked.

"Those things. Don't you see them? They look like little logs. They look like—"

Suddenly, she knew. "Oh God." Righteous horror rose in her throat, and she didn't care how many glances they exchanged. "Oh God."

NO ONE UNDERSTOOD WHY SHE WAS SO UPSET. Noah wouldn't be playing out there for another year. And they were going to clean them all up in the spring. It's all good, Joe kept saying. At least Devin had opened one of their Chardonnays. The sound of the metal cap twisting free of the bottle had an instant calming effect. Even the baby things on the floor didn't bother her so much now that she was sitting on a barstool watching Devin chop mushrooms, her fingers caressing the stem of her wineglass. Erin apparently had become a vegan. He was making a vegan Bolognese.

Maureen, Ruth remembered, had liked a good steak. She hadn't been comfortable with that relationship at the beginning. Not, as Erin automatically assumed, because Maureen was another woman but because she was so much older. Fifteen years. Closer by two years to Ruth's age than to Erin's. And then there was all that drama with her former partner, who nearly got her fired from the university and refused her access to their adopted son. It had seemed a lot for Erin to take on. But Maureen always took such an interest, asking for a garden tour each time she and Erin came to visit, commiserating about Ruth's three miscarriages, her abandoned dissertation, even backing her up occasionally around the dinner table. Maureen, she'd speculated to Joe a few months before the end, might be my closest woman friend.

Now she imagined telling her about the dog shit. And their backyard, she'd say, is full of all this ancient excrement. Maureen would get it, both the lunacy and the horror. She'd had a sense of humour. But Devin wasn't so bad. He was even reasonably nice looking if you squinted away the lumberjack get-up and that ridiculous beard, though there was no denying his legs were short. Ruth lifted her glass with a little smile, and Devin filled it.

Now he was setting the island, placing the knives and forks directly on the damp laminate along with a bowl of cut-up bread and some olive oil on a salad plate. Erin meanwhile kept trying to nurse Noah to sleep. Every time he pulled away, though, lips twitching blissfully, one or both the dogs barked.

"Tired baby," Ruth said.

Erin sighed. "Can you put them outside, hon?"

"Sure thing. Give me just a sec."

"Be careful they don't track that stuff inside," Ruth said.

While Devin was letting Asher and Luna out the sliding door, she poured herself another inch of wine, and one more as he strained the spaghetti

"Okay, hon. We're ready." He brought over a padded bouncy seat with a mobile of cloth sheep and Erin placed the dozing Noah inside.

"We'll see how long that lasts," Ruth said.

Then she remembered a terrible story. How another mother—not someone she'd known well but used to see at Erin's school—had put her youngest in a bouncy seat on the kitchen counter and somehow the baby managed to maneuver it off the edge and had ended up in a coma.

"You don't ever put that thing on the island, do you?"

"No. God. Obviously we don't, Mom."

See, Ruth wished she could say, to Maureen maybe. It doesn't matter what I say.

Devin handed her a bowl of noodles and vegan sauce. In the yard, the two dogs leaped toward one another like lovers in a field. Then Luna lowered herself onto her haunches and deposited a fresh log.

Following her gaze, he said, "Fertilizer, Ruth. We're going to grow vegetables."

And Erin snorted. "Yeah, Mom. We'll send you a box."

Devin got down from his stool to fetch the second bottle from the fridge. Ruth drained her own glass in readiness, ignoring Joe's socked toe against her ankle.

"Can you pour me some too, hon?" Erin asked. "Just a taste." She was rocking the bouncy seat with her foot and looking cross, though Devin had been doing all the work.

"You know he might sleep better in his crib," Ruth said, and when Erin didn't acknowledge this remark, "You haven't opened my present."

"Maybe after dinner, Ruth?" Joe suggested.

"It won't take long."

Joe slid down from his own stool and brought the gift bag to Erin who listlessly plucked off the tissue paper, only to cry, "Oh." She held out the blue cardigan and the matching bonnet and booties. "Mom, they're gorgeous."

"I knitted the same pattern for Erin as a baby," Ruth explained to Devin, who for once seemed genuinely interested in what she had to say, reaching out to touch a sleeve.

"Your mother spent hours," Joe said.

Erin pressed a bootie to her cheek. "Thanks so much, Mom. I love them."

And although it could have been the wine, Ruth suddenly felt forgiven. And not just for that thing she'd said last summer, for other offences too that she no longer clearly remembered but knew had been piling up for years like dead leaves behind a shed.

"Here, let me take them so you can eat your dinner," she said, tucking the layette back inside the gift bag again, then tossing the bag toward the couch, not caring when it landed on the floor.

"So what have you decided to do about work?" she asked. "Or are you thinking of staying home?"

And just like that, the conversation wobbled. "I'm not saying one is better than the other." She noticed the three of them now exchange a glance.

"Actually, I'm going back to school."

"Med school?"

"Grad school," Joe quietly interjected.

"She's planning to do a master's in counselling," Devin added.

"Oh. Good to know."

"I didn't tell you, Mom, because I knew you wouldn't approve."

"I don't know what you mean, I wouldn't approve."

"Well, you haven't exactly approved of very many of my choices." Erin was using the same cloyingly pedantic tone that Joe always used to explain how something Ruth had said was out of line.

"I approved of Maureen," Ruth offered up, because she'd been thinking about her.

And Erin gave a brittle laugh. "Yes, that's true. You two were kindred spirits."

She knew she'd said the wrong thing again, but felt wronged herself too. Maureen and Erin had been together ten years. Naturally, she'd made an effort.

"Maureen was emotionally abusive, Ruth. Toxic." Devin was using that same tone now. "She belittled Erin constantly, made her feel she could do nothing right. So what exactly are you saying? That you liked Maureen better than you like me? That you wish Erin was still with her?"

"Let's talk about something else," Joe said. "She didn't mean it, Devin. She's just had a little too much to drink. We're so happy you've found each other, and that this young fellow has come into our lives."

And as if recognizing his grandfather's voice, Noah opened his eyes.

"Finish your wine," Ruth said to Erin. "I'll take him."

"No, he's fine, Ruth," Devin said. "I'll pick him up if he starts to cry."

The barstool turned out to be higher than she was expecting. "You made the dinner," she said, gripping the edge of the island to disguise her stumble.

"I can take him, Mom."

But Ruth was already reaching under the mobile, unfastening the bouncy-seat straps, sliding her hands under his arching back. "Shh," she whispered, for Noah was crying now. "Grandma's got you."

Safely upright, she began to bounce him as she'd watched Devin do. She couldn't remember the last time she'd soothed a baby. It all came back, of course, especially once she'd repositioned him so that his stomach lay flat against her shoulder. His cheek was so soft against her neck, his breath so sweet. She'd known that if she just could hold him, everything would be okay. And he seemed to be settling. The more she bounced, the more he quieted right down.

"Careful, Ruth," Joe said.

She turned from his voice.

"Mom!"

"Shh, it's going to be okay, sweetie," she said, rocking him side to side.

"Mom, please."

"Ruth," Joe said in that tone she hated.

But it was too late. Her foot had caught in the ribbon handle of the yellow gift bag. She could feel herself lose balance. Then there was nothing she could do. She was going to hit the floor. She was going to hit it on the same side with Noah, his little head protected only by her hand, the hand already gripping him too hard.

*

DAYLIGHT HAS BEGUN TO SEEP IN AROUND THE blinds at last. From the bed, Ruth studies two towers of

Rubbermaid boxes wedged against another mirrored closet. Some are stuffed with spiral-bound notebooks from Erin's courses, others with coats and jeans and squashed shoes. One curiously with skeins of yarn and pieces of fabric from what appear to be a series of never-started craft projects along with cellophane packs of buttons, pipe cleaners, and googly eyes—which makes her own eyes well up again. He's okay, Joe said when he came upstairs, turning on his side in the bed to face the door. For a long time before that, she lay awake listening to him fill the dishwasher, deal with the dogs, hold whispered conversations on his phone, but she must have passed out at some point because she didn't hear Erin and Devin returning from the hospital.

The whole of her right side aches. Her head too. In her purse is the bottle of extra-strength codeine from her night table at home. She lifts her side of the duvet. Joe doesn't stir, so she shifts her feet onto the floor. He must have removed her skirt, though she still has on her blouse and the black tights. Squatting in the gap between the bed and window, she rummages through the purse for the pills and swallows them dry, two capsules. Then she feels around for her skirt and stumbles into its crumpled circle.

On the stairs, all she knows is that she needs to get away—from Joe and his accusing weight on the bed, the sensation of Noah's little head in her hand. She wonders if Erin will tell him how his grandmother dropped him as a baby. Not that Grandma, she imagines Erin telling him. Your other one, the one we don't see as much. My mom. She feels woozy again and clutches the railing. It wasn't supposed to be like this. Why have all the nice things she's ever done just floated off, leaving only this ugly mess of unintended cruelties? Gazing down at her winter boots, she considers simply walking out the door, then remembers that her car keys are in her purse. She doesn't have the energy to search Joe's parka for his. Anyway, where could she go?

So, instead, when she reaches the bottom, she carries her boots and coat to the kitchen. Under the sink, she finds a box of garbage bags as well as some stray used grocery bags. Already feeling calmer, she opens the cutlery drawer and, when she can't find what she wants, the drawer below. This lower one has no dividers and at the clanging of its contents, the two dogs rustle in their crates. She pulls out a couple of carving knives, swishing them sword-like in front of her, before settling on a solid-feeling pie server. Luna gives a hopeful yelp when she places a hand on her crate, but Ruth merely zips up one boot, then the other.

The air hits her first, like a clump of icy leaves, and for a second, she almost can't breathe. When she reaches the doghouse, she slips a grocery bag over her left hand (she's glad she thought of that) and with the other shoves the pie server into the ground. It's slow work. The turds number in the hundreds. They have no smell and feel silky through her bag glove, oddly phallic, like the banana pops she used to freeze for Erin in summer. Some, it turns out, are not logs at all but petrified mud puddles that she can only peel off by sticking the pie server all around the edges. She has to kneel to do this, which hurts her side again. The cold, though, is invigorating, and her headache mostly gone, and after about twenty minutes the garbage bag so full she has to drag it.

Behind her now, she sees no turds at all and nearly claps her hands. Then she hears barking and turns to look toward the deck. Joe and Devin are standing just inside the sliding door. Over his striped pajamas, Joe has on the sea-green sweater she knitted for him thirty years ago when she was still just learning. It never fit right, the torso too wide and the arms barely extending to his wrists, yet he's refused to let it go, even driving to the Sally Ann once to reclaim it from a garbage bag. Joe knocks on the glass, mouths words, while Devin dressed in his same clothes from yesterday sips from a coffee mug. Ruth gives them both a cheerful wave, then stoops for another log, a fresh one this time so only semi-frozen.

When she next glances up, her daughter's there too, Noah in a snow-white sleeper in her arms. As Ruth watches, he cranes his whole face to find the light: something Erin used to do. In those first heady weeks, when Ruth could still barely believe that this beautiful creature was really hers to love and care for, she'd wander about her and Joe's first apartment for hours, showing her new baby their two faces in the mirror, looking with her over the edge of the couch at the budding trees. And as soon as Erin could sit upright in a nest of pillows, she'd take her outside to the back garden where she tugged up grass and flowering clover, staring at each piece on her soft, little palm as if it were made of spun glass.

Erin passes Noah to Devin, then slides the door open.

"Mom." She doesn't sound angry, just tired. "You don't have to do this. Come inside."

Ruth kneels again. The turds on this section are much smaller and round, arranged in pyramid-like piles. She pries the tiny balls apart, then tries to roll them into the bag, but they keep escaping like marbles. Her head is throbbing and her kneecaps through the thin skirt sticking to the ground. If Erin asks again, she might go inside.

But this time when she looks up, Erin's gone.

And now Devin and Noah are turning away too, receding into the warm hollow of that untidy suburban home where she knows she will never be fully welcome, and only Joe is left.

"Ruth. Please." He steps onto the slushy deck in his sock feet. "Come in." He seems to be trying to scoop up the air with his hands. "It's all good," he says.

Little Girl Lost

ON A FOGGY SEPTEMBER MORNING IN 1960, DEBBIE stands by a French door in an old house in Saint John watching a young couple talk on the side lawn. The man in the couple is her future brother-in-law and the woman his wife of two years, Aline. Although she's wearing heels, Aline's head barely rises above the socked clubs in the golf bag perched between them. She's petite. Also, she's from France, which Debbie supposes explains not only the loveliness of all her clothes (today a simple cream shirtdress accentuating her tiny waist and slim ankles) but also her penchant for melodrama. Before dashing outside to plead with Wally one last time, she asked in her glamorous accent, Aren't you hurt too, Debbie? And when Debbie replied, No, not really, Aline exclaimed, I will always be hurt.

Yet the father-and-sons golf game could hardly have come as a surprise. Bob reminded Debbie about it at least five times on their drive over from Halifax. It's tradition, he said, which he says a lot. In Debbie's family, there are no traditions, only chores, and even these her mother has let go of, too sad most days to do much besides reread her favourite novels in bed. By her early teens, Debbie was used to coming home to find her father in her mother's flowered apron peeling potatoes or waving about burnt fingers because he'd accidentally touched the hot bread pan again. This was before Edgehill—the worst year of Debbie's life, the year she discovered how gauche she was simply because of coming from the south shore of Nova Scotia, where her only access to nice clothes was the occasional trip to Yarmouth, her father complaining all the way about how you young people think money grows on trees. Also, at fifteen, she had horrible acne. Not the nearly undetectable whiteheads of the other girls but huge red blotches that spread together underneath her skin like measles.

But so had Bob. Before a Saint John High dance once, he got so desperate he scraped off all his pimples with a horsehair brush that had no business touching a human head let alone a face. He told Debbie this as a funny story, although it was one of those moments in the lead-up to his proposing when she felt a deep sympathy. Not that she needs to spend every second with him, like Aline with Wally. If Bob goes away, to one of his Army camps or to visit his family in Saint John on his own, she feels wretched and writes teasing letters berating him *(Dearest idiot!)*, but she can't imagine making such a fuss over a golf game. Why shouldn't the boys spend a day whacking little balls around with their dad? It isn't as if they're marching off to war.

Then with a clink of shame she remembers: Aline saw her best friend murdered by a German soldier. This was one of the first things Bob told her about his French sister-in-law, along with what a fabulous cook she is and how she couldn't wait to share housekeeping tips with her new little sister. A bayonet was what the soldier had used, though Bob was vague about the other details. Standing at the French door with her cup of cold coffee, Debbie knows that this terrible thing that happened should make her feel sorry for Aline, but somehow it just makes her sorrier for herself. For being too young and out of the way to have experienced much of the war beyond blackout curtains and a game with dolls under her bed she called The Germans are Coming, for bringing all the wrong outfits to Saint John (today a heavy plaid skirt and sleeveless blouse in boarding-school white) and being so flat-chested that she has to stuff her bra with tissues, and for this niggling fear, like a run she keeps dabbing with a nail polish brush, that her marriage, like so much else about her, isn't going to measure up.

Wally has bent his large blond head closer to Aline's tiny, darker-haired one. Now their foreheads touch, and Debbie feels sure he will give in and stay behind, that they'll embrace like Nico and Andrea from *In Love and War* and advance toward her arm in arm. But he only hoists the golf bag over his shoulder and hurries toward the driveway where his father and Bob are waiting in

Bob's car. Leaving Aline to stride back across the grass all alone in her beautiful dress.

OVER BREAKFAST, A PLAN HAD BEEN HATCHED for the three girls to go window shopping while the boys play golf and then have lunch at the Admiral Beatty Hotel. But Aline has a headache and needs to lie down, so Bob's mother has suggested they save that outing for another day and invited Debbie to join her on a delivery to an old family friend. The drive along the Kennebecasis River is very pretty and they can talk about the wedding.

Tall and big-boned with a freckled face that has begun to collapse into her neck, Belle-Mère is capable and no-nonsense in a way that Debbie finds reassuring, yet she also has an air of sadness. Her only daughter died at twenty, Debbie's age. She was diagnosed as a baby with a rare blood disease and Belle-Mère devoted herself to keeping her alive, taking her to Toronto and Montreal and Boston to see specialists, chasing down donors for her weekly blood transfusions. Bob, as a result, might have been a little neglected—this is Debbie's theory at least. He would never criticize his mother. Or anyone else for that matter, including the old university friends who openly flirt with her, getting her to sit on their laps at parties or kneel on their shoulders in the lake, asking what she's doing with a dolt like Bob. She teases him about this sometimes in letters too.

Once they're settled in the Oldsmobile—known as Madelon after a song from the first war (they're a family of nicknames)—Belle-Mère warns her that the man they're calling on might seem a little odd. He was married to one of her nieces, but two years ago she died of cancer, and he's not doing well.

When Debbie asks, Belle-Mère grimaces. "Drink." Archer, she explains as they drive past a large brick hospital, was a bomb aimer with the RCAF but came back a broken man. Constance, her niece, saved him. They were both older when they met, in their mid-thirties, and from what Belle-Mère knows, the marriage was a happy one, although Constance was always sickly. "Did I mention he's an artist? He showed great promise before the war. But the new pictures—" She makes another face. "I've bought a few, to help him out. Otherwise, he just gives them away to handymen. Or taxi drivers for getting him home smashed from the Air Force Club."

"What are they like?" Debbie asks.

"Disturbing. Some are religious, but too religious if you know what I mean. And others are frankly pornographic. You'll see. They're all over the house. But I don't mean to frighten you, Debbie. He's an odd man but can be quite charming, and we won't stay long."

After this, Belle-Mère turns to the wedding. It's still eight months away and the reception at Debbie's parents' house will be very simple, just tea and sandwiches (her parents are Baptists), but there's still her trousseau to discuss and her china patterns. Belle-Mère would like to take her to the Birks uptown to see their Royal Copenhagen collection. The Flora Danica pieces, which feature hand-painted wildflowers, would make a lovely set for everyday. (Debbie's parents' only china set is from Woolworths and most of the pieces are chipped and scratched. Her mother cried when she phoned to say that Bob proposed.)

The Kennebecasis *is* very pretty and much wider than she's been expecting, with several densely wooded islands. Belle-Mère tells her that the road they're taking used to lead to the airport before the airport was relocated farther east. Most of the houses are quite modest, ramshackle even, yet every so often a grander one rises from around a bend. One of these reminds her of the top of an old-fashioned paddleboat. It's a yacht club apparently. Others are summer places dating back to when this area was primarily a retreat for wealthy Saint Johners trying to escape the fog.

"That's all changing now," Belle-Mère says, waving vaguely at some woods on the other side of the road where a new subdivision is to be built on the decommissioned runway.

At last, they turn onto a private gravel road lined with birches.

"Here we are," Belle-Mère announces as the house comes into view. This too is not what Debbie's been expecting. "It was Constance's, her money," Belle-Mère explains. "But as you can see, he can't keep it up."

And getting out of the car, she can see that great patches of its white paint have peeled off while much of the elaborate gingerbread trim on the wraparound porch is broken and several of the plantation-style shutters cling by a single hinge. On one side of the house (really more a mansion) is a large garage with yellowed windows and a mossy, caved-in roof. On the other, a scraggly blue spruce towers over the remains of a flower bed. What she can't see is the river. The property is too overgrown.

Belle-Mère reaches into the backseat of the Oldsmobile for a box of pantry items, which Debbie notices includes a jar of the brandied peaches they had over ice cream the night before and, even more confusingly, a bottle of wine.

As she presses the bell, Bob's mother smiles conspiratorially. "Ready?" When no one comes, Debbie offers to hold the box and Belle-Mère peers through one of the squares of dirty glass that line the doorframe. "Well, I guess we could leave it," she says. "I just worry about animals."

She gives the bell one more firm push. This time, there's a small, distant shuffling noise, then the sound of a dead bolt being dragged across. On a threadbare Oriental carpet stands a little girl, one of the prettiest Debbie has ever seen, with a puff of white-blond hair and very pale blue eyes, made more striking by the extreme lightness of her eyebrows and lashes. The child is barefoot and, although it's nearly eleven o'clock, wearing a white flannel nightdress, quite grubby, under a pea-green cardigan with large buttons.

"Lyca!" Belle-Mère exclaims. "I thought you'd be away at school. Debbie, this is Archer's daughter. Do you remember me, Lyca? It's Great-Aunt Elizabeth. And this is Debbie, my son Bob's fiancée. Can you tell your daddy we're here?"

Belle-Mère has half knelt to deliver this speech at eye level, but the child won't look at her, staring instead at the lowest door hinge. She must be very shy, Debbie decides. Possibly also a little touched in the head—it's the nightdress and something vague or absent in those curiously pale eyes.

When she finally speaks, her voice is surprisingly low. "My daddy's not here."

"Will he be home soon?" Belle-Mère asks. "Do you want us to stay until he comes?"

"You can stay," she says, then turns and skips back inside.

"Well, I never. She's supposed to be at boarding school. Do you mind, Debbie, if we wait just a little while?"

"No, not at all," Debbie says. Already she can see herself regaling them all at the dinner table, confident and amusing in a way she hasn't managed so far. *While you were out whacking little balls around, Belle-Mère and I had quite an adventure!*

Bob's mother leads her through a cavernous front hall into a shockingly disgusting kitchen. It appears to have been recently remodelled—is much more modern certainly than Debbie's parents' kitchen or the kitchenette she shares with her friend Natalie on Lucknow Street—but the candy-pink counters and matching Formica table are hopelessly cracked and stained. Not to mention loaded with dirty dishes and crushed-together glasses, empty wine and gin and whisky bottles, and all these jars of foul-looking water with paintbrushes and tarnished knives and forks sticking out. Debbie has to shift aside a bunch of beer bottles just to settle the box on the table, and she can't help noticing all the mouse droppings scattered about confetti-like.

Belle-Mère, mouth grim, is already at the sink, carefully stacking its contents on the checkered-tile floor so that she can turn on the faucet.

"Debbie, dear," she says. "Why don't you see if you can find Lyca?"

SHE FINDS HER IN A ROOM GRAND ENOUGH TO BE a ballroom, though clearly used mainly as a studio. The walls are crowded with framed pictures while newer works have been piled up against armchairs and chesterfields and stacked on top of not just one but two pianos. As Belle-Mère warned, the pictures are disturbing, especially the religious ones. It's the rapture on his figures' faces. Even Jesus looks unhinged. More like an inmate of a provincial mental hospital than the gentle saviour of Debbie's Baptist Sunday school lessons. She doesn't like his flowers either. The stems are overly long, the heads oddly hairy or drooped over as if they've been shot dead. In one, the stem is a naked woman with wide hips and small translucent breasts. In another, the flowerheads turn out to be smirking children.

Lyca sits in a small yellow-striped armchair near one of the pianos. She has to be aware of Debbie but remains very still, her eyes fixed on the far wall, although her cheeks twitch occasionally like a squirrel's. The chair appears to be her father's painting one. On one side is a folded-out TV tray and on the other what Debbie recognizes as a conga drum. Both their surfaces are littered with tubes of oil paint and charcoal-crayon stubs, crusty rags, art books, overflowing ashtrays, empty liquor bottles, more dirty glasses. The bent shade of a pedestal lamp has been twisted to face a paint-splattered easel, and a cord snakes across the carpet to a television set on a wheeled metal cart. On top of the television is a small brown sculpture of a naked man.

"Hello again," Debbie says. "I'm Debbie."

"I know," the child says.

"How old are you?"

Lyca allows herself a furtive glance. "How old are *you*?"

"See if you can guess."

"Sixteen."

Debbie groans. "Surely I don't look that young. I'm twenty and engaged." She sticks out her hand with the engagement diamond. "Okay, it's my turn. I say you're six."

"Nine."

"Well, I guess we're even," Debbie says, though the child's real age unnerves her. Could she be malnourished? Certainly neglected—that flannel nightdress can't have been washed in weeks. "Where's your school?" Thinking Ontario because Belle-Mère said *away*.

"Windsor, Nova Scotia."

"No. Really? You're at Edgehill? That's where I went, for grade eleven anyway. Do you like it?"

Lyca looks at her straight on this time and shakes her head.

"Ha, I didn't either. So why aren't you there now? Hasn't school started?"

"Daddy needs to borrow a car."

"He doesn't own one?" Debbie's own father scrimped and saved for that one year of boarding school and her later three at Dalhousie, but they never did without a car.

"It's broken."

"Where's your daddy now?"

"He had to walk uptown for something."

Debbie, who has a pretty good idea what that might be, makes a show of gazing about the room. "This is a very big house."

THE TOUR BEGINS WITH THE DRUMS. THE ROOM contains about a dozen, all but the smallest put into service as makeshift tables, their bodies brightly painted and latticed with rope or simply polished a rich brown. They were her mother's, Lyca tells Debbie. The pianos too. She points at a charcoal drawing on the wall of a woman's face. A sick, hollowed-out face framed by limp pieces of hair, the eyes so thickly drawn they resemble coals.

"That's her."

"Oh," Debbie says.

There are more pictures of Constance, looking in all of them on the verge of death, if not already gone. Also several nudes that feature a man, small-boned and slender with pale, trim buttocks, and at least one self-portrait. She wouldn't say he's handsome exactly. His chin is too round, and his ears stick out, but his eyes are certainly intense. He seems to be staring at her, challenging her to feel as he does. The whole room, she realizes, not just the art but the cigarette burns in the expensive carpet and the mess generally, an expression of his disordered grief. In the pictures of the two of them together, he and Constance stand off in the distance beside a body of water or among enormously tall reeds that remind her of the stems of his ugly flowers. One, however, hanging above a stained chintz chesterfield, shows them much closer-up, and they appear to be devouring each other, their heads merged in a splatter of frenzied colour and their genitals only partly concealed behind muscular coils of vegetation.

For a second, she considers covering Lyca's eyes, then reminds herself that the child lives here. Some of the time anyway. "Don't let those Edgehill girls get to you," she says.

Lyca shrugs, but Debbie senses they probably have. "They think I'm stunned, that my name is stunned."

"I think it's beautiful," she lies.

"It's from a poem. Do you want to hear?"

Before she can answer, the child has begun chanting in her gravelly voice some very strange rhyming verses. At first, all Debbie catches is something about a prophecy and a desert becoming a garden mild. Eventually, though, a sort-of story emerges. Lovely Lyca, seven summers old, has wandered far from her mother and her father. Now she's resting under a tree and all these beasts of prey gather around to watch her sleep: leopards and tigers and a lion who bows his mane of gold to lick her bosom. And now a lioness is removing all the little girl's clothes and the other beasts are conveying her away to some caves. And that's the end. No going home, no ever seeing her parents again—just a cold rock floor. As Lyca recites this last stanza of her poem, Debbie's struck again by her almost otherworldly prettiness, yet also by a quality of nervous tension that has crept into her face, suggesting what she might look like at thirty, or fifty. Especially if life is not kind to her. And it will not be kind, Debbie feels sure of this, and she experiences a sudden urge to pick the child up and run.

Instead, she says, "Well done. Aren't you clever to learn all that by heart."

"I had a kitten, but she died."

"Oh dear."

"A cougar killed her."

"Oh dear. Are you sure it was a cougar?"

But the child is leading her by the hand out of the studio and across the hall. They stand for a few minutes in a banquet room with a lot of blackened silverware on display. Then Lyca leads her into the kitchen, where Belle-Mère offers them each a biscuit from the pantry box and asks if Debbie doesn't mind waiting a little longer (No, of course not, she says). Then up the wide spiral staircase to the second floor, which includes yet another ballroom, this one with floor-to-ceiling windows that confirm the existence of the river beyond the tree line. And then, although Debbie yanks on her hand, trying to get her not to, into her father's bedroom.

The room stinks of booze and cigarettes and something else, cat piss or just regular piss, while its velvet drapes have been loosed from their brass holders, making it hard for her to distinguish anything much beyond the bed.

"Come on." Lyca has started bouncing.

His sheets are yellowed, flecked with ash, and in the middle of his bed is a long trench-like dip. "I don't think your daddy would like that."

But Lyca keeps insisting, so Debbie lowers herself to the edge of the jolting mattress. Behind her, she can feel the slope of that man-sized dip. She grabs one of the carved bedposts to stop herself from sliding into it. She doesn't want to turn and look at it either, but then she does and immediately she pictures him there, lying on his side watching her. No more obscuring vines.

She yanks herself upright. "Ready to go?"

But Lyca is bouncing on all fours now.

With every thud of mattress and responding squeal of bed springs, Debbie expects the child's father to appear in the doorway. The thought gives her a queer excited feeling. At the same time, she can't stop handling his things, running her fingers along the top of his dresser over the used handkerchiefs and spilled coins, the empty cigarette packs, a crumbling robin's nest cradling three petrified blue eggs. Whisking away loose husks of dust.

This, she reflects on the way back down the curving stairs, is why they need us. To keep them civilized, keep them sane. And thinking of her fiancé and how he too simply empties all the contents of his pockets on his dresser, she feels a returning clarity, a sense of purpose, of mission even. Yet fluttering underneath a kind of terror, like the first time she saw Bob without his clothes and thought, I can't go back now.

THE FOG THEY APPEARED TO ESCAPE BY DRIVING inland has caught up, or maybe it was here all along, only hiding. On the verandah, Debbie can't stop rubbing her arms. She also can't stop glancing up the gravel road, thinking a man with a bottle-shaped paper bag is about to emerge out of the birches. What can Belle-Mère still be doing in there? Waxing the kitchen floor, polishing all his silver trays? For the first time it occurs to her that there might be something unseemly in Belle-Mère's interest in the husband of a dead niece. Lyca picks up a fallen slat from one of the shutters, taps it against the gingerbread railing. She looks back to see if Debbie's watching, then hops off the front steps and points at the blue spruce.

"That's where my mother's buried. And my kitten too."

Debbie claps a hand to her mouth. She's picturing a woodcut from her mother's old hardcover edition of *Wuthering Heights*: Heathcliff in his black greatcoat digging up Cathy's grave, eyes ablaze. "He didn't make you watch?"

But Lyca has leaped over a dead rose bush and now is running, still barefoot, down the side of the house, leaving Debbie no choice but to chase after her in the good kitten-heel shoes she put on when she thought they were going to the Admiral Beatty for lunch. The back of the property is much wilder. Great waves of dogweed get in her way, each one higher and unrulier than the last. Also sumac bushes, their scarlet seedheads raised like bloody daggers. Lyca seems headed toward the river, though all Debbie can see of her through the dense brush is the occasional patch of flannel or green wool. Her shoes are getting ruined, so she stops to take them off. But her nylons keep catching on bits of stick and then she stubs her toe and has to lean against an ancient oak matted with vines to rub it, after which she can't see Lyca anywhere.

Eventually, she comes to a body of water, though not the river. A stagnant, algae-coated pond, surrounded by Queen Anne's lace and goldenrod and stands of thick-stemmed woodland angelica. And Lyca still nowhere to be found.

Debbie calls her name. "Come out, come out, wherever you are," she teases. If Lyca's hiding like her father's smirking flower children, she makes no sound. "Okay, see you later, alligator! I'm going back now."

Only she can't. All the little doubts have taken hold at once. What is she even doing here? She barely knows these people. And they don't know her. They're all so happy for Bob for having found her (Such a sweet girl, Such a dear), but they have no idea what she's like inside. How she's constantly thinking about other men, wondering what it would be like with one of his friends.

With this Archer even.

A car door thuds. From the road come voices. Belle-Mère's. Then a man's, flat and self-possessed. Debbie rubs her arms again. Her shoes, hooked over a pinkie finger, bang against her exposed flesh. Her feet are soaked. She thinks of the kitchenette in her Lucknow Street apartment. How when she and Natalie get home from dates, they peel their nylons off and drape them over the backs of their chairs, then rest their tired feet on the table, put the kettle on.

Then out of nowhere Lyca grabs her hand.

The child's is rough, the nails sharp—yet so are Debbie's. Where can they run? Down to the river and along the bank until they reach a town. Or, better yet, a bus depot, where Debbie can use the money in her skirt pocket to buy them tickets to Montreal or Toronto. Where she can find a small apartment above a store and herself a job, maybe in this same store. Enroll Lyca in a nearby school. Write Bob a letter.

Just wedding jitters, that's all this is. Still, he'd understand. He sees the good in everyone. It's what she cannot bear.

They've reached the side of the house and she can see the blue spruce standing guard over its garden grave, hear the voices more clearly now. Including to her surprise a third, higher and brighter than the other two.

"Where's Lyca?" this other little girl sings out.

The hand in hers twists, struggles to pull free, but for a moment Debbie won't let her go. She sees herself bend to swoop her up, then turn and run toward the river,

Lyca's arms clasped now around her neck. And when the girl gets too heavy, she sees herself set her down on the bank, and the two of them, hand in hand, vaulting over stones, seeming at times almost to fly.

*

ON A SUNNY AFTERNOON IN THE SPRING OF 1976, Deborah (she dropped *Debbie* after her divorce) stands outside a new art gallery in uptown Saint John, deliberating whether to go in. She and Jerry are in the process of buying a winterized cottage off the Sand Cove Road, and she's just come from the Antique Centre where she put his name on a Nisbet mahogany card table, circa 1840. Her taste in furnishings still owes much to her former mother-in-law, although she hasn't seen the inside of that house she so admired all those years ago since Belle-Mère's death in '64 (she drove out there once and was shocked to discover the side lawn paved over and a torn basketball net hanging from the French door). Jerry's taste, or rather his ex-wife's, runs more toward corduroy couches and teak coffee tables and hideous brass flower sculptures from Birks. But he's coming around to antiques, in part she suspects because he enjoys the haggling with dealers.

At the bell, the gallery owner glances up but resumes his conversation with three young people, which suits Deborah, as she only wants to browse. She's bought a few watercolours at auctions, pastoral landscapes in gilt frames, but no *real* art yet, and she's curious to see if any of Archer's pictures are here. They've naturally shot up in value, and she's read all the profiles. Knows things now, like how on bombing missions over Germany he carried William Blake's *Songs of Innocence* in his breast pocket, and how he had a solo exhibit in Toronto once where not a single painting sold.

The papers rarely mention Constance, but with experience, Deborah has come to realize that what spooked her in his house that day was a truth about love. *Real* love. How it tramples over everything. Cannot be reasoned with or pretended away, put back in its bottle or left to run its course, as Bob for a long time hoped that hers and Jerry's might. Deborah has left her children for this kind of love, and Jerry's done the same, although for five awful months, right after she'd told Bob, he went back to his wife. But that's in the past now and they're living openly together at last, for the time being in a one-bedroom apartment over a new shopping mall that Jerry helped to finance, yet soon to move into their own home, which she plans to fill with beautiful things. Things that express the perseverance of their love, their deeply shared life to come.

Nothing on the crowded walls of the new gallery seems quite right, though, and she's about to duck out when the owner calls, "I'll be with you in a minute, ma'am."

And now she's stuck because his customers, two long-haired, bearded men in their twenties and a short blond girl, all wearing ragged bell-bottom jeans and sunglasses and stinking of weed, are saying long good-byes and blocking the doorway. The girl's sunglasses are the granny style with small round, orange-tinted lenses, and at one point she smiles at Deborah. At least she sucks in her lips. A little insolently, Deborah feels.

"So," the gallery owner says after they're gone. He's closer to Deborah's age but also what Jerry would call a peacenik type. His cheeks above the beard are plump and acne scarred. "Is this your first visit?"

She answers yes and asks about Archer.

"Well, you're in luck. One just came in. It's only a sketch but very striking."

He places a large paper bag on the counter, slides out a framed picture and carefully unwraps its layers of soft wrinkled brown tissue. As the image emerges, Deborah recognizes not only the frenzied pencilwork but also the two nude figures locked in an embrace.

"That's him and Constance."

The gallery owner appears impressed. "You knew Archer?"

"No, but I met the daughter once."

"Ly-ca," he says, lingering fondly over each syllable. "Well, you just missed her. That was Lyca who was just here."

"Really?" Deborah darts to the glass door, but naturally the blond girl and her companions are long gone. "What a coincidence. I didn't recognize her. I haven't laid eyes on her since she was seven or eight. Somehow, I thought she'd moved to Toronto after he—"

She feels embarrassed suddenly. All that she knows about Archer's final descent into alcohol-fuelled madness, as well as his teenaged daughter's decision to take what money was left and run, having come from the papers. The girl seemed so different, not nearly as pretty. The wide-legged jeans not a flattering style on such short legs.

"She was in Toronto for awhile but most recently Wales."

"Wales? What was she doing there?"

"Well, I don't really know."

"Does she come back often?"

"She still owns the house, so sometimes."

"I worried about her when she was little," Deborah confides. "That time I met her, he'd left her all alone. His car was broken, so he walked to the liquor store. It must have taken him a couple of hours each way. I was with my mother-in-law, my *ex*-mother-in-law, and we waited and waited, but he just never came back. Luckily, a neighbour drove up with his little girl and we left her with them."

"That was probably the Sullivans. They looked out for Lyca when they could and would have adopted her if Archer had been open to it." Then, seeming to become embarrassed himself, he adds, "Of course, he loved her too much to ever part with her."

Deborah doesn't know what else to say. She makes some appreciative noises about the sketch, but it isn't the kind of thing she can imagine Jerry liking and she isn't sure she likes it either. The lovers' embrace doesn't seem natural. She thinks of her and Jerry's stolen afternoons together, how they clung on motel beds. One time he sat her on his lap and cupping her small breasts from behind so that they filled his hands whispered through her hair, I couldn't live without these. And she twisted herself around and pulled his body so close she couldn't tell which was his heartbeat and which hers. In Archer's sketch, only he clings. Constance could be a large rag doll. Her arms and legs dangle over the sides of his lap and her gaze is glassy and unfocused as if she doesn't know or even care much where she is. It seems less a testament to love than an acknowledgement of its futility.

"I'll have to think about it," she says.

"Would you like me to hold it for you, ma'am?"

"No, that's okay."

RELEASED BACK INTO THE SUNSHINE, SHE CAR-ries on toward her and Jerry's apartment, watching vaguely for Lyca. One of the young men had an expensive-looking camera strung around his neck on a bootlace, so the girl was likely giving them a tour. Deborah smiles thinking of the conga drums. They must have headed down to the waterfront, though, or uphill to the old burial ground, and she realizes she's relieved. She doesn't think there's any chance that Lyca would remember her. Still, she didn't like the way the girl looked at her, as if she guessed all about Jerry and the one-bedroom and found Deborah's ideas about love bourgeois, uptight. She pictures the three of them fooling around together in that filthy house. A tangle of pale, hairy legs, Lyca kneeling suddenly on those same old yellowed sheets to light a joint.

She hasn't driven out that way yet and probably won't. Not because she isn't curious to see the house again but because Jerry's family home happens to be in the subdivision on the old airport lands, and she worries she might be tempted to continue to that address. Early on, when they'd been in the one-bedroom just a few weeks, she made the mistake, after too many martinis, of asking him about the ones who came before her. Thinking she could handle it, that she had a right to know, that it might even turn her on, since she was the last, the one he couldn't do without. Instead, all the bits of information he threw out that night—their first names, their hair colours (so many other brunettes!), how long each affair lasted, and all the ways he kept it from his wife—had only clawed at her certainty and would still, if she let them.

Darting across King Street and up the wide concrete steps to their building, she reflects that love, the deep sexual kind she has with Jerry, is like faith in God. It's always being tested, requires its own form of zealotry. Also, the way to finding it is not always clear or easy. That day in Archer's house was an early sign that the life she'd been brought up to think she wanted—nice man, nice house, nice well-adjusted children—would never satisfy her. What she'd been yearning for was more akin to rapture, or as she'd put it in a letter once to Natalie, *passion and affection and friendship all flowing through one man's strong body*. Yet she went ahead and married Bob. And even after she and Jerry fell in love, she would often find herself worrying over his endearments, the precise words he'd used, clinking these together in her mind like rosary beads until they came to mean only what she needed most.

The shopping mall under their apartment doesn't have much in the way of shops: just a Woolco and a Radio Shack and a tobacconist with a window full of pipes. And it's always so gloomy in here, despite the plants. All fake, of course, although the leaves of the palm trees scrape the ceiling. Deborah takes this same route, past the huge fake palms and the fountain with its eerie blue- and pink-lit cones of water and huddled smokers, several times a day, could walk it with her eyes closed and sometimes almost does. Only awhile longer, she tells herself. Yet today even a glimpse of the elevator doors brings her down. The ugly brass knocker on their apartment door, a fat little man holding up a pint glass, even more so. For Jerry, the one-bedroom is the perfect love nest. He can sneak home in the afternoon for a quick fuck (she tries to be back by two), mix himself as many martinis as he likes at night. But she doesn't know what to do with herself when he's gone and especially Thursday evenings when he drives to Millidgeville to take his four children out to dinner.

Her own three fly over from Halifax one weekend every month, and she spends the days before in a happy daze of baking cookies and planning little expeditions. But the manic drone of Saturday-morning cartoons and her children's occasional rudeness, the sleeping bags and clumps of clothing on the living-room carpet get on Jerry's nerves, and lately her twelve-year-old daughter, who's oversensitive and not getting along with Bob, has begun phoning not only after school but just as they're sitting down with their cocktails or to a gourmet dinner that she's spent hours on. What's wrong now? Jerry will ask when she emerges finally from the bedroom, and she can only shrug. Her daughter's need a quicksand that if she doesn't tread carefully could, she knows, devour all her happiness.

Fumbling for her key, then slipping off her sandals in the entranceway, Deborah so expects to hear the phone again that its plaintive ring is already echoing in her brain. To calm her nerves, rattled as well from seeing Lyca after all this time, she glances at her most recent purchases for Sand Cove Road. The bigger pieces of furniture are being held until the move, but the watercolours in their gold-painted frames are neatly stacked against the living room wall, while at the end of the tacky brown corduroy couch that Jerry bought before she came (and will not be going with them!) stands an antique spinning wheel and three large ceramic jugs, as well as a bag of the pink-and-green-leafed fabric she plans to sew into a bed skirt.

She closes her eyes and imagines her feet sinking into their new bedroom carpet, as thick and soft as moss. Imagines walking past the bathroom with its mint-green sink and matching bathtub and the two smaller rooms where her children will sleep on their monthly weekends (and hopefully longer in the summer). Then down the steep, attic-like stairs, glancing into the tiny cottage kitchen Jerry has assured her they'll remodel before long and gliding through the living room to the sunroom, where at the end of the day they'll curl up on their new chesterfield, with its intertwining blue and yellow chintz flowers, and sip red wine and share the papers while the waves below them gently crash. And so reassuring is this vision, so comforting, like a long-desired homecoming after a perilous journey, that for a moment she almost doesn't hear the ring.

How the Smoke
Gets in Your Eyes

MY POLICEWOMAN HAS FOUND A CIGARETTE BUTT just inside my bedroom door. Do I smoke, she wants to know.

"My husband did," I tell her from my armchair. "Three packs a day. Marlboro Reds when I first met him and later Rothmans. King-size. The newsroom was like an opium den." I can tell she's confused so add, "He's dead."

Coming into the sitting room, she says, "I'm sorry."

"It's been twelve years."

She nods, holds out her palm. "This must belong to your intruder then?"

"Well, the least he could have done is step outside," I say, and this time am rewarded with a grim smile.

She's warming up to me, as people tend to do. No doubt because at this age I pose so little threat, though

I'd like to think that it's my witty repartee. At first, she flustered me, asking all those questions at the door and then appearing to not quite believe my answers, but I sense we'll be trading funny stories before much longer, that she'll notice my paintings, ask about Ted. Still, I would have expected her to put on special gloves before handling the cigarette, to seal it in a Ziploc bag like on the British police procedurals I watch with my granddaughter, Molly, who's fifteen and obsessed with serial killers, so am a little disappointed when she simply tips it onto the table beside my chair.

At least she's taken photos of the boot prints. Jane would not be happy with me if I let the police come and go without collecting any evidence at all. My daughter hasn't been able to stop by yet due to an important meeting with a client, though in a way I'm glad. Jane always raises the temperature in a room, Ted used to say, and today my instinct is to keep the thermostat low, not make a fuss. The bedroom print is the most complete. A man's size 9, she's told me, although she didn't measure, only eyeballed it as she slid her phone back inside her jacket pocket. He must have been standing there awhile, she said. She didn't add *looking in*, but that's clearly what he was doing. Looking in at me, and now it appears smoking.

The rest are just bits of tracked-in dirt, which I may have wrecked shuffling in my slippers to the bathroom. I haven't mentioned the glass. It's probably too late. When I saw it on the counter, I let myself believe the glass was Brenda's from when she was here last and, although it looked empty, squirted in some Dove, rinsed and set it in the rack with my dishes from the night before. By then I'd noticed the computer, or rather the absence of computer, and was trying to convince myself there was nothing wrong with this, that I'd only misplaced it somehow—printer, cords, and all.

Once I started back across the sitting room, of course, I saw my purse upended on the couch and all its contents strewn about the cushions. The new upholstery from the nineties is worn and burnt in places, but you can't get this kind of quality anymore. That's what I'm always telling Molly (Don't let your mom get rid of this couch when I'm gone), though I can't remember when I last sat on it before this morning. The view's different from what I'm used to. In my armchair, I see out to the street with its trees and passing cars and people, but the couch faces inward, and I couldn't not glance up occasionally while hunting for my wallet. That's how I noticed the yellow nicotine stains on all my paintings, the dust as thick as a sheet of dryer lint on poor Ted's books. For a moment, feeling about the frayed fabric, I felt like an intruder too.

What a dump, I thought.

We bought the house soon after we got back in '65. Kevin was three and Greg just starting to toddle about. It's what's known as a Craftsman bungalow: tan stucco with a covered porch supported on wide columns of mortared beach stones and, inside, three smallish bedrooms, a sitting room and galley-style kitchen with a dining nook, just one bathroom. Ted had rejoined the paper, this time as an editor, though the salary was not much more than he'd made in Toronto as a cub reporter and we were grateful when his mother offered to cover the down payment. He always meant to renovate the attic crawlspace, to move one or both the boys up there, build me a proper studio in the backyard, but he wasn't much of a handyman, let alone a craftsman, and we couldn't afford a carpenter. The house, as a result, always felt a little crowded, especially after Jane arrived in '69. Arguably a little dark as well, since we never thought to paint the woodwork and there's a lot of this if you count floors and ceiling beams along with baseboards and windowsills and all those built-in bookcases that were such a selling point for Ted.

We had different expectations in those days. That's what I try to explain to Molly, whose bedroom in her mother's new house is as big as all three of mine combined and who can't fathom how her uncles could have bunked in together all their teenage years. It was cozy, I say. When your mom and her brothers came home from school, I'd put aside my paints and we'd have tea, right here, at this same table, just like you're doing now with me. And Uncle Kevin and Uncle Greg never spent much time in their room anyway except to sleep. They were out with their friends playing road hockey or shooting baskets or doing their homework or watching TV.

But Jane has nothing nice to say about this house. It was like growing up in a wooden box, she tells Molly. A smoky wooden box, which is a dig at her dad. He did smoke too much around us. Nerves, I can see now. He was an anxious man in his way, irritable at times, especially when he had something on his mind or couldn't find his lighter. Even after he'd lit up, his fingers would keep fumbling about at his side as if he were still fondling the thing, and then half the time, he'd forget he had a cigarette on the go and pull another from the pack. Predictably, he's smoking in all our family photos. Look at your grandpa, Jane will say when I'm showing Molly the albums. Waving his death stick about as usual in his babies' faces. There's one I took near where we lived that year on Walmer Road that she always comments on. Ted, shirt sleeves rolled, tie askew, is holding up Greg in his diaper and a little white sailor top. Big grins, the both of them. Only this time my husband's stuck his death stick in our baby's mouth. We thought it was funny, I suppose.

When did I start asking him to step outside?

Probably not until the eighties when there were all those reports on the nightly news about second-hand smoke. The other risks were well known by then, not that people seemed to care that much. It helped that they could still do it almost anywhere. They smoked at the office and in bed, on planes and buses, in grocery stores and shopping malls and university classrooms and hospital wards and waiting rooms of all kinds, dropping their butts into metal ashtrays built into the arms of seats or sconce-like ones attached to walls or in public fountains or the gutter.

I might have too if I hadn't been playing tennis in the hot sun the one time I tried it with a girlfriend. Later, just thinking about the taste could make me retch. But I never minded the smell. To the degree I even noticed (it was so pervasive then, like lemon-scented floors or leaded gasoline), I liked it, though the smell got into everything. Into our food, my paints, the bedding, the children's toys. Even the diapers I boiled on the stove and hung outside to bleach dry in the sun. As for Ted, he could soak an hour in the bathtub. He could pummel his armpits with deodorant, slap on half a bottle of Old Spice, squeeze dab after dab of Brylcreem on his hair. His whole body reeked of Rothmans. And that's probably why I liked it, because the smell got so mixed up with his.

Jane wishes I would stop reminding her, but Ted was my only lover. I didn't have sex with anyone before him, and I certainly haven't since. For awhile after Toronto, he would sneak home when the boys were both at nursery school and surprise me in my painting clothes. Even the sound of footsteps on the porch could get me wet. We couldn't keep that up forever, especially as the paper and his health began to fail. Yet I still get an occasional spark of that old longing. Usually after a dream in which I find him in this house again, leaning up against the counter with that clunky brass General Motors ashtray of his mother's he used to cart around when he couldn't find the others, or blowing ash off a record before he settled it on our wooden turntable. Miles Davis. The Beatles, Joni Mitchell. The Platters for old times' sake. But it doesn't last very long. By the time I'm fully awake, the feeling's gone. And then I'll remember the way I felt lying with him afterward. How he'd automatically reach for his lighter. All right, sweetheart. Patting the hand with the lit cigarette on my hair. Gotta go.

My policewoman has been checking window latches. Now she tries the kitchen door and notices a framed watercolour on the wall. It's of Jane at five or six, wearing a white blouse and tartan skirt and rocking her Raggedy Ann.

"Are you an artist?" she asks.

"Not really. I dabble, or I did. My hands are too stiff these days to hold a brush." I hold my fingers up for her to see. "Arthritis."

They weren't as bad yet when I stopped. But Ted was. After he grew too weak to hold a razor, I'd shave him every morning in bed. Tiny white hairs flecking the sheets no matter how carefully I draped the towels. You shouldn't have to do this, he'd say. He didn't think I should have to help him in the bathroom either, though I often think about his penis, how soft and delicate it felt in my hand—newborn, as his whole being seemed to me those last few months. No one tells you this: how much a person changes at the end. Becoming suddenly older, frailer, yes, yet younger somehow too. The boys by then were both married and living in Ontario, and Jane was busy establishing her practice, Molly still a toddler. And afterward there were his financial affairs to settle, letters to write, a memorial service to arrange. For awhile, I kept the brushes and charcoal pencils in their pretty pitchers on the table. But once the kids bought me the new computer, there wasn't room, and I wasn't sure anymore that I really wanted to. So I asked Brenda to put everything away in a cupboard, though now I can't remember which one.

"That's too bad," my policewoman says, still studying my painting. "You were good."

"The little girl is my daughter, Jane. She has her own daughter now, named Molly."

She nods. "And this I'm guessing is where the computer was." She's pointing at a lone dust-free square on the table. "I assume it's password protected?"

"Do you mean do I have a password for it? Yes. But I think there might have been a sticky note on the side with my banking one on it."

"You shouldn't write them down, you know."

"I know. Jane's always telling me that too, but I can't remember if I don't. I used to write them down in a little book, but then I lost it."

"You could try a password manager."

I have no idea what she's talking about but try to look as if I do.

I COULDN'T FIND MY WALLET ANYWHERE ON THE couch, but the phone thankfully was lodged in the gap behind the middle cushion. My intruder must not have noticed it slip down. Or maybe he didn't care about an ancient Motorola that Molly claims I couldn't give away.

I sat for a moment feeling the Motorola's reassuring weight through my nightdress on my crumpled thigh, then pressed my daughter's name. "Jane," I said. "It's your mother."

"I know, Mom. You're in my contacts, remember?" Just before eight: never a good time. "So what's up?"

"Well," I said. "It looks like I might have had a visitor in the night."

"Hmmm. Another mouse?"

"No, actually a man."

"Sorry, a *what*?"

As I explained about the computer and my ransacked purse, I could hear Molly in the background asking, What's wrong with Gran? and felt my heart rate start to race. No, I didn't think anything else was missing. No, I didn't hear a thing and had no idea how he got in.

"Oh my God, Mom, he could have hurt you."

"Oh. I don't think so."

"Absolutely he could have. There are men who target elderly women, you know." And when I didn't respond, "Sexually."

"Well," I said, hoping for a little levity, "I was wearing a Depends, which might have been a turn-off."

"Jesus, Mom. This is *serious*. Have you called 911? You've got to call them the second we hang up. And you realize you're going to have to call the bank too, right? And the insurance company. At least they should pay for a new computer. Oh my God, my God, we've *got* to get you out of there."

And into a home is what she means, though not a nursing one. An assisted-living home where I'll still have my independence. It'll only be harder later, she keeps reminding me. Better to make the move while you still have the energy. And aren't you lonely on your own? Wouldn't it be nice to make some new friends your own age, to have a trained caregiver do the cleaning and prepare your meals?

I have a lot of history in this house, I tell her. And I have Brenda.

But Jane doesn't think that highly of Brenda anymore.

"Mom, are you listening?"

"I'm just going to get dressed first and put a few things away."

"No. Call. Right now. And don't touch a thing, okay? Not a *single* thing."

When Brenda comes, she always makes a point of pausing to admire this one sketch I did of Ted that used to hang in his office at the newsroom until he accepted the early retirement package in '98. What a handsome man, she'll shout over the drone of the vacuum. Or to make me laugh, Such a babe. She does miss a lot of dust and puts things away in the wrong places and sometimes places where I never find them. And a few times she hasn't come at all, when she's said definitely she would. But I appreciate the little touches. How Brenda always folds the first square in a new roll of toilet paper so that it points down like in a fancy hotel she cleaned for once and how as soon as the snow melts, she brings in cuttings of dogwood and forsythia and deep-purple lilac so the whole house smells of spring.

Her husband, she's confided, was handsome too. But he had a poison in him. When she finally got herself and the boys out of there (stuffing a few clothes in grocery bags, trailing the school bus until it stopped out front a neighbour's she could trust), she was so afraid he'd come after her that the four of them lived in her car for weeks. Daryl, who was only six, would wake up screaming in the night, convinced his dad was rattling the backseat handle trying to get in—which is why she thinks he struggles so much now with drugs and other troubles. You were lucky, she said one day gazing at that sketch of Ted. He does look handsome in it. Tall and loose-limbed with those long brown sideburns, the plaid tie he always wore in the seventies flung over the shoulder of his sports jacket and the smoke billowing about his face. Yes, I said. I was.

Jane groaned when I told her that. Oh right, my sainted father. She thinks I've put Ted on a pedestal, can see him now only through a soft romantic haze. During her divorce, I made the mistake of telling her the real reason we left Toronto. I meant to show I understood what she was going through. But she seized on the part of my story that differed from her own. How could I be so sure he didn't do it again? All those late nights and weekend newspaper conventions, the girl-reporters he was always bringing along on family outings. Carol, didn't I remember Carol in her string bikini, how he spent hours at the lake teaching her to swim? Or the one who called him all the time at home but wouldn't leave her name? Which gets her on to her father's insensitivity more generally. How he chain-smoked in the car and refused to pull over if she or one of the boys felt sick, then got me to clean up the mess because the smell of vomit made him gag. How he only supported my painting so long as it didn't interfere with dinner. Never encouraged me, for instance, to go to art school. Never built that backyard studio he'd promised.

I don't point out the obvious. That if I'd left him, I wouldn't have her and Molly now. That I can't imagine my life without my girls. I also don't tell her how close I came. How for years the thought of that young woman in the doorway of our flat on Walmer Road, her short brown hair and sulky prettiness (No, you don't know me, but your husband does), could catch me unawares, like a knife pressed up against my throat. And how, as soon as I could breathe again, I would put the baby in the stroller—first Greg and later Jane—walk briskly to the bank and get the teller to write out the balance in our joint account, then stand there in that blur of strangers with the slip of paper in my hand. Instead, I say it happened a long time ago, and her father made amends, giving up that good job in Toronto and coming back here for my sake.

What a martyr is her stock response.

After I hung up with Jane, I called 911 and spoke to a very nice operator who told me not to worry, she'd have someone stop in to make sure I was okay. Then I heaved myself up with the help of the couch arm and reached for my bedroom door, noticing the boot print but not the cigarette. I straightened the duvet the best I could, then opened the top drawer of my dresser and took out underpants and a greying bra, hauled my nightdress over my head, and rolled the adult diaper down my legs. For years, I slept so lightly, sitting up each time Ted coughed, but since he's been gone, I sink to the bottom of a silent well. And last night was the same.

Opening other drawers, I pulled out my favourite brown corduroys and a pink turtleneck. I wrestled on the turtleneck, which squeezed my face like a balaclava but once I got my arms through felt as comfy as I'd hoped, then leaned against the bed to inch on one pantleg and then the other. At some point in the early 2000s, Ted moved out of this room into the boys' one. It made sense with his sleep apnea and later his emphysema, the oxygen tank he needed when his COPD got worse, all those pill bottles and inhalers crowding the nightstand, and I find it difficult now to imagine how we ever managed together in such a tiny space.

So much about the way we used to live is hazy to me now. But Ted is not. That's what I wish I could explain to Jane, that I see him so much more clearly now. That all that other stuff just blows away—or at least for me it did. But when I try, she always wants to know what it is exactly that I see, and I can't find the words, these too seeming to have blown away as well. Of course, in the moment, it's hard to know what you should do: whether to leave or stay. A marriage rarely feels so open-and-shut when you're still in it. Even Brenda, who had far more cause, for a long time wasn't sure. There seemed to be risks to both, she's said, and her husband made all the usual promises. It's like you're squinting at your life, she told me once. Trying not to see too much. Which made me think of that old Platters song Ted always hopped the needle to. How the smoke gets in your eyes.

MY POLICEWOMAN HAS SAT DOWN ON THE END OF the couch closest to my chair.

She takes out a notebook and a pen, speaks more gently than at the door. "So, Mrs Davies, I need to ask you just a few more questions." And my heart does a little skip because of that empty glass I washed. "First, you say nothing's missing except the computer and your wallet, and that there were only a couple of twenties in that?"

"Yes."

"No meds, for instance? You're not on OxyContin or Ambien?"

"No, no. Just cholesterol pills. And some for high blood pressure. Now that I think of it, the bathroom cabinet might have been a little bit ajar."

"Okay, good to know. I'm still confused by how he got inside. There's no sign of a break-in and you said you didn't hear anything? You're sure you locked up before bed?"

"Yes."

"So, what I'm wondering is if someone might have got hold of your key. Is there anyone other than your daughter and your granddaughter who has a copy?"

"Just Brenda."

"Brenda?"

"She comes in every couple of weeks to—" I feel myself becoming vague again.

"Clean maybe?"

"Yes."

"And this Brenda, she wouldn't have given it to anyone?"

"Oh. God, no."

"Do you have her number handy so I can call her? Just to check if she's noticed if her key is missing?" She readies her pen.

"Well, I'm not sure. Let me think." This time I welcome the vagueness in, let it billow out between us. "My daughter might. She's a lawyer. Can I ask her to call you?"

She closes the notebook. "Absolutely."

I tell her then about the time Ted set his favourite sports jacket on fire with his lighter. It burned a big hole in the pocket, I say, but he loved that jacket so much that he just made sure never to carry anything important on that side. She has a funny story about a pocket too. Her husband had planned to propose to her at a beautiful lake, only on their hike there he lost the ring through a hole in the pocket of his fleece. When I ask hopefully, did they? she smiles. Yes, on the way back, between two tree roots. I tell her about being at a wedding once where the mother of the bride for mysterious reasons tried to move the wedding cake. It did not go well, I say. She advises me to call a locksmith and repeats Jane's instruction about the bank. She'll call if she has any news.

Only after she's gone do I remember the cigarette. I pick it up from the side table and hold it near my lips. I didn't hear a sound all night. No rattling at the door. No running of the faucet, no footsteps. But I might have smelled something. When I woke, I remember now I felt Ted's presence in the bedroom doorway. Nothing distinct. Not like those times he's visited me in dreams, a still-youngish man with long brown sideburns cradling that brass ashtray of his mother's. Yet familiar and sheltering all the same.

While we wait for the tea to steep, Brenda always pours herself a glass of water from the kitchen faucet, because Daryl keeps telling her she should drink more water. But then she barely touches it. He's a good boy at heart, she's told me more than once. He'll turn around, get clean for good, go to college. Maybe even law school, like your Jane. And I'm sure she's right. Just as I know Jane's still grieving, both her father and her marriage, and that Ted didn't cheat on me again—and even if he did, that I forgive him. I wouldn't trade our life together for any other, and at the end I know he felt the same. Once Brenda and I are done catching up, I put her full glass on the counter to dump out later when I wash up the mugs and my old Brown Betty teapot with the broken spout. I'm sure Jane's right about the insurance. As for the rest, it seems a small price to pay for so much love.

Acknowledgements

THESE TWELVE STORIES OWE SO MUCH TO THE loving encouragement and keen editorial eye of my husband, John Ball. For all, he has been my trusted first and last reader. I could not have embarked on this journey without him. I am also deeply grateful to my daughter, Hilary, and sons, Jack and Peter. They were still in school when I began writing fiction, but I quickly came to rely on their astute story advice, and their enthusiasm for this new direction in my life has meant the world to me.

My mother, Judith Brannen, died before most of the stories in this book were written. I am so thankful for her early feedback, especially on "Maeve," and for her belief in me as a writer. My father, John, died after most of them were completed yet before there was a manuscript. The delight and pride he took in my work given the number of drunk fathers in these stories is a testament to his sunny and giving nature. His favourite was "Old Growth," which has always touched me.

Heather Marmura, Teresa Doucet, and Lee MacLean read many drafts. Their insights into life and art have made these better stories, and I will never forget their generosity. Others along the way who also generously read and commented include Peter Rothfels, Sue Sinclair, Dawn Lefurgey, Jeramy Dodds, Douglas Vipond, Don Gillmor, Colleen Kitts-Goguen, Marla Force and Oliver Zielke, Linda McNutt, Megan Woodworth, Rabindranath Maharaj, Kerry-Lee Powell, Mark Jarman, Clarissa Hurley, Cynthia Daffron, Melinda Lefurgey, Randall Perry, Barry Callaghan, Ros Calder, David Huebert, and Lizzie Derksen.

My childhood friends Maria West, Nora Perry, Caroline Nunn, Wendy MacGregor, and Kristina Nicoll helped me recapture the texture of seventies-and-early-eighties Halifax, while Sally Dibblee, Kate Rogers, Anna Cameron, Louisa Baird, Paula Emery, Sheila Brooke, Margaret Watson, and other friends in Fredericton and beyond were always there to celebrate each small publishing success, whether over social media or in a conga line to "Paradise by the Dashboard Light."

A special thanks to my brothers, Peter and Gavin, for gracefully putting up with the occasional borrowing from our family stories, and to my Alward cousins, Marc and Dominique.

Earlier versions of "Old Growth," "Wise Men Say," "Hyacinth Girl," and "Little Girl Lost" appeared in *The New Quarterly*. "Cocktail," "Maeve," and "Pomegranate" were originally published in *The Fiddlehead*, "Hawthorne Yellow" in *untethered*, "Orlando, 1974" in *Prairie Fire*, and "Bear Country" in *Exile*. I am very grateful to the editors of these journals for their support, especially *TNQ*'s Pamela Mulloy. I'd also like to thank Craig Davidson, Ross Leckie and Kathryn Taglia, Dilshad and Nicholas Macklem, *Best Canadian Stories*, and the Journey Prize. A generous Creation Grant from the New Brunswick Arts Board helped me to finish my manuscript, for which I am most appreciative.

I have been so impressed by the care and professionalism my first book has received from everyone at Biblioasis. Vanessa Stauffer steered it through production and marketing with sensitivity and good humour, and I can't imagine a more perfect cover than Ingrid Paulson's gorgeously allusive design. My heartfelt thanks to Dan Wells, to my excellent copy editor Chandra Wohleber, and to my wonderful publicists, Madeleine Maillet and Emily Mernin.

Lastly, I wish to express my gratitude to my editor, John Metcalf, who believed in this book when it was not much more than a couple of stories and whose passionate championing of the short story form over many years is an inspiration to all who try to see by the flash of a firefly.

PHOTO: MARIA CARDOSO GRANT

LISA ALWARD'S stories have won
The Fiddlehead Prize and the Peter
Hinchcliffe Short Fiction Award and
have appeared in *Best Canadian Stories*
as well as *The Journey Prize Stories*.
She grew up in Halifax and worked for
several years in literary publishing in
Toronto before moving with her family to
Vancouver and ultimately to Fredericton,
where she lives with her husband, John.
This is her first collection.